Race Against Time

Driving to the Rainbow Ranch to model for the first TV commercial, Nancy found Tony Traynor and his film crew already there. As soon as her makeup had been applied, she was ready to start.

A stable boy led a shining big black stallion out into the summer sun.

Tony said, "I thought Stormy would be a good horse to start with. Is it all right with you, Nancy?"

"Oh, yes! Isn't he a beauty!" She patted and soothed the restless animal. "Okay, Stormy, here we go!" With that, Nancy lithely mounted him.

She was no sooner in the saddle than the big black thoroughbred began to buck and kick wildly. As he galloped and snorted, it was all Nancy could do to hang on.

Stormy was out of control, and Nancy was losing her grip!

Nancy Drew Mystery Stories

Available from MINSTREL Books

NANCY DREW MYSTERY STORIES®

66

NANCY DREW®

RACE AGAINST TIME

CAROLYN KEENE

A MINSTREL® BOOK

PUBLISHED BY POCKET BOOKS

New York   London   Toronto   Sydney   Tokyo

This novel is a work of fiction. Names, characters, places and incidents are either the product of the author's imagination or are used fictitiously. Any resemblance to actual events or locales or persons, living or dead, is entirely coincidental.

A MINSTREL PAPERBACK *ORIGINAL*

A Minstrel Book published by
POCKET BOOKS, a division of Simon & Schuster Inc.
1230 Avenue of the Americas, New York, NY 10020

Library of Congress Catalog Card Number: 81-21918

ISBN: 0-671-69485-5

First Minstrel Books printing August 1987

10 9 8 7 6 5 4 3 2

Printed in the U.S.A.

RACE
AGAINST TIME

Contents

1

Sinister Happenings

"Nancy, are you really going to hunt for that missing racehorse?" Bess Marvin asked.

Nancy's blue eyes twinkled as she and her two friends rode through the woods. "How can I, when I haven't even been asked to help on the case?"

"But I thought the *River Heights Record* asked you," George Fayne said. She was Bess's slim, tomboyish cousin.

"Oh, that was just an editorial." A valuable thoroughbred had been stolen, and the local newspaper had advised the police to call in the famous sleuth, Nancy Drew. "A racing mystery might be fun," Nancy added, "but no one's consulted me."

"Oh, oh! That reminds me," George exclaimed.

1

But her words were cut short by a scream from Bess as her horse reared and whinnied in fright.

A dark-colored cat had just darted across the bridle path, startling Bess's mount. The pretty blond girl, who was plump and rather timid, struggled to keep from falling out of her saddle.

"Whoa!" she wailed, reining her horse to a halt. "Now we're in for bad luck!"

"At least you didn't take a spill," George teased. "I'd call that pretty *good* luck!" Trim and athletic, she was proud of her boy's name and inclined to make fun of her cousin's nervousness.

"That isn't a black cat that crossed our path, anyhow," Nancy remarked. "It's a tortoise-shell."

The beautiful little creature, whose dark fur was streaked with brown and orange, paused to stare at them with its jewel-like topaz eyes before disappearing into the underbrush.

"You're right," Bess said sheepishly. "Even so, it did give me an awful scare!"

Nancy smiled and, to allow her blond friend time to catch her breath, turned to the other girl. "What were you reminded of just before that cat ran out in front of us, George?"

"You said that no one had consulted you, Nancy, which made me remember that someone did leave a message for you." George groped in the back pocket of her jodhpurs and pulled out a folded paper. "Remember after we saddled up and you two were ready to start, I had to go back to your car to get my riding crop? Well, this was tucked under your windshield wiper. I'm sorry that I forgot about it."

Curious, Nancy took the paper that George handed her. It bore the name *Nancy Drew* scrawled in pencil. Opening the note, she read:

IF THE RIVER HEIGHTS RECORD TRIES
TO HIRE YOU, TELL THEM NO DEAL!
YOU MIGHT GET HURT!

Seeing the expression on her friend's face, Bess asked, "Is anything wrong, Nancy?"

Instead of answering, Nancy showed the other two girls the message. Bess was shocked. George looked up angrily. "Is this creep serious, Nancy?"

The girl sleuth shrugged. "It may be someone's idea of a joke. I'll give it to the police." Smiling quickly, she added, "Come on! If we're going to meet Ned's film club and see where they're planning to make their movie, we'd better not stay here talking."

The three eighteen-year-old girls nudged their horses forward again. It was a sunny Saturday afternoon, and they were on their way to an old house known as the Grimsby Mansion, deep in Brookvale Forest. Nancy's friend Ned Nickerson had persuaded a local realty firm, which owned the house, to let his college film club use it as a setting for their amateur production. Nancy had agreed to play a role in the film.

"Tell us about the movie, Nancy," Bess pleaded. "Is it really going to be a vampire drama?"

"Well, it's not really meant to send chills down anyone's spine," Nancy smiled. "Ned made up a tongue-in-cheek story, so to speak. It's sort of a spoof of scary horror films."

"I'll bet it's a riot," George grinned. "Did he write the scenario himself?"

Nancy nodded. "He had to. The club plans to enter the film in a contest. But the project got off to a late start, and they needed a script in a hurry in order to qualify. So Ned dashed one off."

She added that another student, named Lenny Arthur, had also written a script, but the club had chosen Ned's.

"It's too bad he didn't write a mystery," Bess said. "Then you could have played the detective!"

Nancy, an attractive titian-haired girl, was the daughter of a prominent River Heights attorney, Carson Drew. Her keen mind and natural interest in people gave her a flair for solving mysteries. Sometimes she helped her father when he was called upon to handle puzzling law cases.

"Actually, there's a small mystery connected with the mansion where the film will be shot," Nancy told her two friends.

"Don't tell us it's haunted," said George with a mischievous glance at her cousin, "or Bess will be afraid to go near it!"

Bess responded by making a face.

"Don't worry," Nancy reassured her. "I'm sure no ghosts will pop out at us! The mystery is whether the house is really unoccupied. When Ned came out yesterday to look it over with the realtor, Mr. Ullman, they both got the impression that someone had been in it recently."

"How come?" George asked. "Were there signs of a break-in?"

"Not really. That's part of the mystery. The house was locked up as usual, and yet it looked as though a few things had been moved around inside and some of the dust covers dragged off the furniture."

Bess gave a little shiver. "The place may not be haunted as you say, Nancy, but that sounds spooky enough to me!"

As the girls rode on along the bridle path, the Grimsby Mansion came into view through the trees. There was no denying its sinister appearance despite the bright sunshine dappling the forest greenery all around it.

A weatherbeaten, gray Victorian mansion, the three-storied house had gables and turrets and gingerbread trimming around the eaves. The realtor, Nancy confided to her friends, had told Ned that the house was over a hundred years old.

"It looks it!" George commented.

Several cars were parked in the broad, weedy courtyard area between the mansion proper and its stable and carriage house at the rear. Scattered about was a small group of people who were talking.

"There's Ned!" Nancy exclaimed as a tall, athletic young man in jeans and a T-shirt waved to the trio. She smiled and waved back.

An A-student at Emerson College, which was located in another state, Ned had decided to take a summer course in filmmaking at Westmoor University near River Heights. His enthusiasm for it had led him to form a film club with other summer students, and it was also Ned who had sparked their interest in the movie contest. The prize to be awarded by a photographic manufacturer would help to buy equipment for the club.

"Who's that fascinating-looking man with Ned?" Bess whispered to Nancy.

6

"I don't know. I've never seen him before."

Though middle-aged, the man was youthful in appearance. His silver-blond hair contrasted with his tanned, bold-featured face. He was wearing a light cotton sport jacket, navy polo shirt, and slacks.

"Hi, girls!" Ned greeted the trio as they reined in their mounts. "This is Mr. Tony Traynor, the famous cinematographer."

Nancy was thrilled as Ned introduced the girls, one by one. "I loved your films, *Morning Star* and *City of Dreams*, Mr. Traynor," she said as they shook hands.

He smiled back. "Thank you. The critics were kind, but neither film made much money, so I'm forced to spend my time shooting television commercials. May I say in turn, Miss Drew, that I admire your talent for solving mysteries."

Nancy blushed.

"Mr. Traynor's been kind enough to give our club some pointers on making movies," Ned explained.

While they were talking, the eight other young people belonging to the film club had gathered around to listen and be introduced to the new arrivals. Nancy had already met some of the members, including a girl student named Gwen Jethro and her boyfriend, Lenny Arthur. Lenny's script had been the one to lose out to Ned's.

7

"Have you learned your lines yet?" Gwen questioned Nancy. She sounded eager for a chance to criticize the Drew girl's performance.

"Not yet," Nancy replied. "But I've played in some productions by the Footlighters, and I think I'm a fairly quick study."

The Footlighters were a little theater group in River Heights. Gwen's lip curled scornfully.

"Huh!" she sniffed. "You'll find performing in front of a camera a lot different from flattering your ego with that little hick group!"

"As a matter of fact, the Footlighters are a remarkably fine group of players," Tony Traynor said quietly. "I've seen some of their shows."

"Oh, really?" Gwen replied.

Instead of being put out by Mr. Traynor's rebuke, Gwen Jethro seemed pleased to have caught his attention. She was carrying a round bull's-eye mirror, which was to be used in the group's amateur movie to show that a vampire casts no reflection.

Feeling the noted director's eyes on her, Gwen whirled away airily, holding the mirror as if to study her own reflection while she practiced her range of dramatic poses. She pretended to be unaware that anyone was watching, but it was embarrassingly plain to everyone that she was showing off for Tony Traynor's benefit.

8

"That girl makes me sick!" George muttered in disgust, hardly even bothering to speak under her breath as Gwen swept across the courtyard, paying scant attention to the fact that she was walking on the edge of a slope that ended in a dry, rocky creek bed. Gwen pirouetted, suddenly losing her balance!

"Look out!" yelled a young man named Mike Jordan, who was acting as property man.

He ran to help her, but he was too late. The mirror slipped from Gwen's hands and went rolling down the slope!

"Oh, *no!*" Mike groaned in horror.

Without even stopping to think, Nancy flicked the reins and nudged her mount, Black Prince. The beautiful horse bounded forward and, in two strides, went streaking down the slope. With perfect timing, Nancy swung out of the saddle and scooped up the round mirror in one hand before it could crash on the rocks.

Cheers and applause went up from the onlookers.

"Nice work, Nancy!" Ned cried, clapping.

"That's one of the finest displays of natural horsemanship I've ever seen!" Traynor declared.

"Thanks," Nancy said, handing the mirror to Mike and wishing everyone would stop making a fuss over the trivial incident. But she saw that the cinematographer was eyeing her thoughtfully.

"You know, Miss Drew," he said. "I'm about to shoot a television commercial that calls for a girl in riding costume on a horse. Would you be interested in doing such an assignment?"

Nancy was startled. "It's nice of you to ask," she said with a hesitant smile, "but I doubt that I could do a very professional job."

"Let me worry about that," Traynor retorted. "I believe you could do a splendid job!"

"Well, I'd like to think about it if I may," Nancy murmured.

"Look at Gwen Jethro!" Bess whispered to her cousin. "She's green with envy!"

"And it's all her doing," George said and giggled.

Ned interrupted to suggest that they go through the house to see the various rooms in which the movie scenes could be staged. Then the club could begin its cleanup.

"A lot of the furniture has been carted away over the years," he explained, "but there's more than enough for our needs."

Taking out a key provided by the Ullman Realty Company, Ned unlocked the massive front door and led the way into the vestibule of the mansion. The real-estate firm had arranged for the utilities to be turned on, so there was adequate lighting even though the shutters had not yet been opened.

A musty odor of dampness, dust, and wood rot pervaded the mansion, and the carpeting was threadbare, but Nancy could not help admiring the marvelously carved woodwork of the stairway and paneling. Ancient dust covers still draped most of the furniture that remained. Even so, she could see that some of the items had once been of fine quality.

"Ooh, this place even *smells* like it's full of ghosts!" Bess declared.

"It could certainly do with a good airing if that's what you mean," George said with a grimace.

Their voices echoed hollowly through the half-empty rooms. Some of the group found themselves tiptoeing, as if afraid to disturb the spirits of the old house. But the more adventurous, like George Fayne, plunged boldly ahead of the rest.

"This place will be perfect for a vampire film!" Nancy congratulated Ned.

"It's certainly full of atmosphere," Tony Traynor agreed, brushing aside a cobweb as they passed.

Suddenly, a startled cry rang out from the dining room just ahead on their right.

"That's George!" Nancy exclaimed. The others followed as she hurried to see what was wrong.

"Look!" George said breathlessly, beckoning

11

them closer and pointing to the mahogany table. Words had been crudely traced in the dust that covered its surface:

INTRUDERS BEWARE!
THE PENALTY FOR DISTURBING
THIS OLD HOUSE IS *DEATH!!*

2

Mystery Call

There was a moment of shocked silence as the young people and their guests stared at the message in the dust on the old mahogany table. Then, everyone began to talk at once. Most of them thought it was a joke.

"I bet somebody's having a good laugh at us right this minute!" said a girl named Denise.

"Okay, who did it?" Mike Jordan chimed in, examining the faces clustered around the table. "Speak up!"

His words brought a chorus of laughter. But there were others, Gwen Jethro and Lenny Arthur among them, who thought that the message might mean danger.

"I think we ought to forget about this mansion," Gwen spoke up, looking around nervously at the rest of the group. "Let's try to find another big old house."

"She's right," Lenny said. "Why ask for trouble?"

But Ned pointed out, "There really is no other house around that's as suitable as this. And remember, time is short. I think this is a prank. It's just the sort of message someone would leave in a spooky old house."

"What do you think, Nancy?" Bess asked.

Nancy shook her head with her finger on her chin and a thoughtful look on her pretty face. "I believe we should be careful, but not allow ourselves to be frightened off."

"Come on! Let's finish going through the rest of the house. And then I vote we start picking up the junk on the kitchen floor."

"Good idea," George Fayne agreed. "Let's get busy!"

Tony Traynor, however, clapped his hands for attention. "People, I'd like to stay and help, but I have an appointment in the city. Nancy, I'll let you know about that TV commercial as soon as possible. I'm sure you'll be marvelous and just what the sponsors are looking for. Good-bye, everyone! I'll

14

try to look in again as you get on with your film!"

Lenny and Gwen and another girl were still against the idea of staying in the mansion unless the warning message had been proved to be not serious. So they, too, left.

Even though Nancy and her two friends were not members of the film club, they stayed and helped with the cleaning for about an hour. One of the first chores carried out by the group was to open the shutters and pry up some of the creaky windows to give the old house a thorough sunning and airing.

At last, the three girls mounted their horses.

"Don't forget about the date we made for tonight," Ned called out to Nancy as she and her friends rode off.

"I won't." she grinned. "See you later."

It was already late afternoon when the girls arrived back at the stables, and they started for home immediately. When Nancy finally pulled into the Drews' long driveway, she jumped out of the car and hurried into the house.

Hannah Gruen, the Drews' cheerful housekeeper, turned from a pan of curry sauce she was stirring to greet her. Hannah had been with Nancy and her father ever since Mrs. Drew's death when Nancy was only three years old.

15

"You had a phone call this afternoon, dear," Hannah reported. "It was some man. He said he needed your help in solving a mystery. But he didn't leave any name or number and just said he'd call back."

Any hint of a mystery was always enough to start Nancy's imagination working. "It sounds interesting!" she exclaimed. "I wish I knew what it was all about, but I guess I'll just have to wait until he calls back."

Then Nancy glanced at the kitchen clock. "I have to hurry and get ready, Hannah. Ned's taking me to dinner and a dance at Westmoor University!"

Forty-five minutes later, she was ready and waiting when the college boy arrived. Ned gave an appreciative whistle, and Hannah said, "Oh, Nancy, you look so lovely in that dress! It goes beautifully with your hair!"

Nancy smiled and thanked her.

"Mm, something smells delicious!" Ned exclaimed as a mouth-watering odor wafted from the kitchen.

Hannah's face showed her pleasure at his remark. "You know I'd love to have you two change your plans and eat dinner here."

"That sounds tempting," Ned said, "and thank

you, Mrs. Gruen, but I have a reservation for us at the Lobster House." He looked at his watch, then at Nancy. "We'd better get going!"

Over a delicious meal of seafood, they chatted about Ned's film and how to achieve some of the effects he was hoping for. But when the waiter brought dessert, Ned asked, "Nancy, what do you really think of that message printed in the dust?"

"I'm not quite sure. It was odd the way Gwen and Lenny acted so upset. It was almost as though they were trying to discourage the rest of the club."

Nancy paused, then went on slowly, "Didn't you say Lenny was angry because your script was chosen over his? I wonder—could he have written the message himself?"

"Could be," Ned said. "I'm trying to remember in what order we arrived at Grimsby Mansion. Let's see. I was there first with the key that Mr. Ullman loaned me. Then the two cars with the other club members pulled in, a minute or two apart. About five minutes later, Tony drove up. Then you and Bess and George rode in from the woods."

"Well, that doesn't sound as though Gwen or Lenny had a chance," Nancy concluded. "But I think we'd better keep our eyes open. Maybe those three who left were just pretending to be nervous because they wanted an excuse not to do any work."

17

Over dessert, Nancy told Ned about her mysterious caller who had left no name or number. Both wondered if the call might have any connection with the afternoon's disturbing turn of events.

The gym at Westmoor was cheerfully decorated and it echoed with lively chatter when they arrived for the dance. The band was already set up, tuning their instruments and testing the sound system.

Although Nancy and Ned were greeted by many friends, their attention was instantly drawn to some other guests, notably several members of the film club at Burnside Tech.

"They have entered the movie contest, too," Ned confided with a grin. "They've probably come as enemy spies."

"Okay, mum's the word!" Nancy joked back. "Pass it along."

Soon after the music began, Gwen Jethro and Lenny Arthur danced by. They glanced slyly at Nancy and Ned, then looked at each other as if sharing some private joke.

"Uh—oh," Nancy murmured to Ned. "I bet those two are up to something." But she quickly forgot about their unpleasant smiles as her enjoyment of the evening grew.

On one occasion, however, she danced with young, bespectacled Professor Walter Barnes, who

18

was acting as Westmoor's faculty advisor to the film club.

"I'm sorry you won't be able to play in our film," he said, startling the girl. "I feel sure you would have done a wonderful job."

Nancy looked at him in amazement. "But I thought I was going to."

"I thought you couldn't," Professor Barnes replied with a frown. "I've assigned the role to Gwen Jethro."

He went on to explain that he had been working steadily at his office all Saturday afternoon, trying to catch up on his overloaded schedule, and had discovered an unsigned note on his desk. It said that Nancy would not be able to play in the club's movie as expected because she was going to be in a TV commercial.

"The commercial isn't definite yet," Nancy informed him, "and, anyway, I certainly wouldn't let it interfere with the film."

"So it wasn't you who left the note, as I assumed." The kindhearted professor looked confused and unhappy over the mix-up. "I'll see what I can do, Nancy. Unfortunately, I have just filled out and mailed the entry form for the film contest, and it lists Gwen Jethro as the actress in the ingénue role."

He added apologetically, "I'll check to see if I can change the assignment again. It's rather awkward. You see, I already had to get special permission from the contest sponsors to enter our film club as a contestant after the June 30th closing date. I hope I won't have to disappoint you, Nancy."

The music came to a stop as the band paused for a break. Nancy and the professor were joined by Ned and Sara White, one of the girls in the film club.

Nancy told them what had happened.

"What a mean trick!" Sara exclaimed. "I wonder who wrote that note?" But as their eyes met, Nancy could tell instinctively that there was no doubt in Sara's mind as to who the guilty party was, even though she did not like to say so openly in front of Professor Barnes.

"This is really awful," Ned remarked. "Do you think there's any chance of getting it changed, Professor?"

"We'll just have to see, Ned."

The two girls and Ned walked to the refreshment table, where Nancy discovered Gwen staring at her triumphantly. The look reminded her of Gwen's and Lenny's sly smiles earlier.

"Three guesses who slipped that note on Professor Barnes's desk!" Sara murmured.

Although disappointed, Nancy knew that the

professor would do whatever he could to remedy the situation. Meanwhile, worrying would not help and would only spoil the evening for herself and Ned.

Just then they were joined in the line by Dr. Frieda Davis and her distinguished-looking husband. She was a young, dark-haired computer specialist on the faculty of Westmoor's business administration department.

"Hello, Ned. How did you get on with Mr. Ullman?"

Dr. Davis knew everyone of importance in the local business community, and it was she who had helped to arrange for the use of Grimsby Mansion by the film club.

"We got along just fine, thanks to you," Ned responded. "The club is going to do some cleanup work in exchange for the favor."

Then he introduced Nancy and Sara.

"Dr. Davis, is there anyone besides Mr. Ullman who can get into the mansion?" Nancy asked.

"Not that I know of. The Grimsbys had no relatives, and the place has been vacant a long time. Why do you ask?"

Nancy told her about the threatening message traced on the dusty table top.

"How strange!" Dr. Davis looked startled. "I

remember last year Mr. Ullman said he had discovered some hippies using the house. But I think he changed the locks at that time. He could tell you more about it."

When the couple returned to the dance floor, Nancy said she intended to find out about the hippies. "And let's ask Mr. Ullman if he's had any trouble since then with other intruders in the house."

"Good idea," Ned agreed, but until they were on their way home again, they said no more about it.

However, when they turned onto North Road, which ran along the edge of Brookvale Forest, Nancy glanced out of the window to her right.

To her horror, the sky was glowing red over the treetops!

"Ned, look!" she exclaimed. "That must be a fire! And it's coming from the direction of Grimsby Mansion!"

3

Stolen Winner

"You're right! Those are flames!" Ned declared tensely. "We'd better get over there fast!"

He swung the wheel and turned up the road that led through the forest to Grimsby Mansion. By driving swiftly over the bumpy dirt road, they arrived at the scene in a few minutes.

Nancy's heart sank when she saw that the stable in back of the house was burning fiercely. "Oh, Ned! How can we possibly save it?" she exclaimed.

"We probably can't. But at least the house itself hasn't caught fire yet!"

The creek bed below the slope was dry, but there was an old well on the property. Ned ran toward it and peered down. Moonlight glinted from the scummy, green surface below.

"Here's water!" he cried, and hastily let down the bucket. Before he could crank it up again, though, the distant wail of a siren was heard.

"Thank goodness!" Nancy said fervently. "Someone else must have seen the flames and phoned in an alarm!"

Ned only had time to splash a few bucketsful on the blaze before the fire truck came screaming and rumbling up the forest lane. Hearing its approach, Nancy quickly moved Ned's car out of the way.

The volunteer firemen, who had responded to the alarm from their homes, wasted no time. They dropped a hose down the well and in moments were aiming a stream of water at the burning stable.

Nancy watched breathlessly with Ned's arm around her. The flames dwindled and finally died out. By that time, however, the stable was a blackened ruin. Some of the nearest trees had also been burned, but luckily the coach house, ten yards away, was undamaged.

"What happened?" the fire chief asked the two young people when at last his men began reeling up their hoses.

"We've no idea," Ned replied. "We were driving back from the Westmoor dance and saw the reddish glow over the trees, so we came to investigate."

"Did you see anyone around?"

"Not a soul. But by then the whole stable was on fire, so if anyone did set it, either accidentally or on purpose, he'd have had plenty of time to clear out."

The unfortunate incident cast a pall over Ned's and Nancy's enjoyment of the evening. "What a shame this had to happen!" she murmured on the way home. "Do you suppose someone really started the fire on purpose?"

Ned shrugged uneasily. "To tell the truth, I don't see how else it *could* have happened," he replied. "There's such a thing as spontaneous combustion, I guess, in a barn full of stored hay where heat builds up bit by bit until the dry stalks kindle into flame. But those stables at the Grimsby Mansion have stood empty for years. Why should they catch fire now?"

Nancy frowned in puzzlement. "I can't imagine either, Ned, unless maybe those hippies came back."

Bess Marvin dropped over late on Sunday morning to join Nancy for brunch. "Did you hear about the fire at the Grimsby Mansion?" the blond girl asked.

Nancy nodded as she poured her guest a cup of coffee. "Ned and I discovered it."

"Good grief! Will that spoil things for the movie?"

"I hope not. There aren't any scenes that take place in or around the stable as far as I can remember the script. There's an important night sequence that happens outside the mansion, but I imagine Ned can aim the camera so it won't take in the burned area."

The two girls heard the telephone ringing, and Hannah Gruen presently appeared in the dining room doorway. "It's for you, Nancy," she said. "I think he's the same person who called yesterday."

"About a mystery he wanted solved?"

"That's the one!" the motherly housekeeper confirmed, her eyes twinkling.

"Thanks, Hannah! I'll be right there!" Nancy responded, dabbing her lips with a napkin and jumping to her feet.

"What's up?" Bess asked, shooting a wide-eyed glance at the girl detective.

"I don't know myself yet, but I'll give you a full report as soon as I come back to the table!"

She picked up the receiver and said, "This is Nancy Drew. Who's calling, please?"

"My name is Roger Harlow," said a deep, pleasant-sounding man's voice. "I own a horse-breeding farm out on Aurora Road called Rainbow Ranch. Perhaps you've heard of it?"

"Oh, yes, Mr. Harlow. I've passed it often."

"Miss Drew, I've heard a good deal about your abilities as a detective. Of course, I know of your father's reputation as an attorney, though that has nothing to do with my present call. It happens that I'm in need of a private investigator, and I wondered if you might be interested in taking on the case. For a suitable fee, of course."

Nancy explained that she delved into mysteries as a hobby and in order to help people, but accepted no payment for her work. Then she asked, "What's the nature of your problem, Mr. Harlow?"

Her caller hesitated. "I'd rather not go into details over the phone. But it would give me great pleasure to meet you in person, Miss Drew. Would you care to drop over for tea this afternoon?"

Nancy accepted the invitation. Roger Harlow thanked her and added, "Shall we say three o'clock if that's convenient? Fine! I'll look forward to seeing you."

Bess was bursting with curiosity when Nancy related the telephone conversation. "Wasn't a racehorse recently stolen from Rainbow Ranch?" Bess asked.

"Yes, I believe so. But he didn't say whether or

27

not that was the problem he wants me to investi-gate."

Nancy herself was intrigued by Roger Harlow's call. That afternoon, she drove through the arched gateway bearing the name *Rainbow Ranch* in wrought-iron script and turned up the driveway toward his stately, white-columned house. She found herself as curious as Bess Marvin over why he had chosen to consult her.

A maid answered the door and escorted Nancy to the drawing room. Mr. Harlow appeared a moment later and held out his hand cordially. He was a handsome, tweed-suited man in his early sixties with thinning hair and a ruddy complexion.

"How nice of you to come, Miss Drew! And on such short notice!"

The young detective smiled back at her host. "A mystery is always a challenge that I find hard to resist," she confessed. "But perhaps we'd both feel more comfortable if you just called me Nancy."

"Thank you, I will. Please sit down, Nancy."

Later, when tea had been poured, Mr. Harlow said, "I don't know if Tony Traynor mentioned that Rainbow Ranch is where that television commercial will be shot."

"No, he didn't," the girl said in surprise.

"Actually, it was Tony's call yesterday afternoon

saying he wanted you as the model for the commercial that made me think of consulting you about the theft of Shooting Star."

"That was your racehorse?"

"Yes, my prize two year old. We chose his name because he has a white marking on his left side that looks just like a shooting star." Harlow's change of expression as he discussed his stolen thoroughbred showed how deeply the loss had upset him.

"When was he taken?" Nancy asked.

"On the evening of July 4th. And I'm sure the timing wasn't just by chance!" Mr. Harlow explained that almost everyone at the ranch had been away that evening, watching the fireworks display at a small park down the road.

"Have you received a ransom demand from the thieves?"

"No, not a word of any kind. Which, of course, leaves the question of motive wide open."

Nancy knit her brows in a thoughtful frown. "Wasn't Shooting Star due to run in the River Heights Handicap?"

"Yes, and it wouldn't surprise me if that had something to do with the crime. I think I can fairly say that most racing experts regarded Shooting Star as the sure winner." An angry look flickered over Harlow's face as he added, "At least they did before he was stolen. I'd like to get my hands on the crooks who did it!"

Nancy mused in silence for a moment, reflecting that Rainbow Ranch was on the edge of Brookvale Forest. "Haven't there been a number of burglaries in this area?" she asked. "I mean, from the large estates and country houses all around Brookvale Forest?"

"Yes." Mr. Harlow nodded. "No doubt you've heard the news reports about them. But those were robberies of money and other valuables. Stealing a big, strapping thoroughbred, sixteen hands high, is another matter altogether. I doubt very much that the same burglars would try to make off with a racehorse."

Their conversation was interrupted as the maid came to report a telephone call. "Mr. Traynor is on the line, sir."

Roger Harlow excused himself from Nancy. But a few minutes later, he returned to summon her to the phone. "When I told Tony you were here, he asked to speak to you," Mr. Harlow said with a smile. "I believe he has some news."

Nancy was slightly breathless as she lifted the receiver. "Hi, Mr. Traynor."

"Nancy, it looks as though this television assignment may happen even sooner than I expected," he

30

began. "I've already proposed you as the model to the advertising agency executive who's handling the account. He's enthusiastic about the idea, but first the sponsor wants to see some stills of you. Could you possibly be at Rainbow Ranch again tomorrow morning—say around nine o'clock for some preliminary posing?"

"Of course," she promised, her heart beating a bit faster at the prospect. "I just hope I won't disappoint anyone!"

She heard Tony Traynor chuckle at the other end of the line. "Are you serious, Nancy? They'll flip when they see how perfectly you fit the role!"

The cinematographer added that she would be well paid for her time. But Nancy asked that any pay for the commercial be donated instead to the River Heights Animal Shelter, her favorite charity.

When she returned to the drawing room, she and her host continued chatting pleasantly for a while.

Mr. Harlow said that he would show her the stable from which Shooting Star had been stolen when she came to Rainbow Ranch to pose the next morning. He would also fill her in on the details of the theft at that time. "For now, I'm content just to know that you'll take the case," he said.

Nancy promised to do her best to solve the mystery of his stolen thoroughbred. Once again, she declined to accept any fee for her detective work. But Mr. Harlow insisted that he would at least reimburse her for any expenses she might incur while investigating the case.

As she rose to leave, Nancy gestured toward an oil painting of a beautiful woman, which hung above the marble fireplace. "I can't help admiring that portrait," she told her host. "May I ask who she is?"

"My late wife Cynthia. That picture was painted almost twenty years ago. She died just last spring." From the catch in his voice, Nancy could tell how deeply Roger Harlow had loved his wife.

As Nancy walked toward the fireplace to study the portrait more closely, she was struck by the beautiful jewel that the woman was wearing as a pendant on a silver chain around her neck. "What a magnificent opal!" Nancy exclaimed.

Her host seemed pleased that she had noticed it. "Yes, isn't it?" he murmured. "I bought Cynthia that opal on our honeymoon in Australia, and she always treasured it above any other piece of jewelry she ever owned. We both loved it! In fact, that's how we came to name this property Rainbow Ranch—from the flaming colors of that very stone."

"It's a lovely name and a gorgeous gem!" Nancy responded.

She had barely returned home and walked in the

front door when Hannah Gruen came bustling into the hallway.

"You're just in time, Nancy! Ned Nickerson's on the phone!"

Nancy hurried to take the call, sensing that something serious had prompted it. "Hello, Ned," she said. "Has anything happened?"

"How did you guess? There's real trouble over that fire at the Grimsby Mansion!"

4

Strange Behavior

"What sort of trouble?" Nancy asked, although she could already guess the answer.

"Mr. Ullman's furious," Ned replied. "He blames the film club's carelessness for the stable burning down. He says in all the years the house stood empty, there was no fire. But we were there one day and look what happened!"

Nancy was as dismayed as Ned at the realtor's attitude, but added, "I suppose we should have expected this. It does look bad for us. Ned, can we be absolutely sure it wasn't due to any negligence by the film club?"

"Positive! I told Mr. Ullman that none of us smoke, and there were no matches lit or anything else done that might have caused a fire. I've checked with everyone in the group. Nevertheless, he's threatening to stop us from using the mansion."

"Oh dear, that would ruin everything, wouldn't it?" Nancy declared.

"You bet it would! We'd never have a chance of finishing the film on time. Finding another place to shoot as good as Grimsby Mansion is practically hopeless." Ned sounded desolate.

"Well, it hasn't happened yet, so don't give up. We'll just have to convince Mr. Ullman that the film club wasn't to blame."

"That may be easier said than done." Nevertheless, Nancy's encouragement seemed to have given Ned at least a small ray of hope. "How about having lunch with me tomorrow?"

"I'd love to. And we can talk over what to do."

Monday morning dawned sunny and pleasantly warm, yet not quite so humid as usual for mid-July. After breakfast, Nancy donned a tailored shirt, jodhpurs, and boots, then added a brown belt and brown scarf. Taking her riding crop, she dashed downstairs to ask her father if he would drop her at Rainbow Ranch on the way to his office.

"I'd be glad to, honey," he replied. "Is that where you're stabling Black Prince now?"

"No, Prince is still at the usual place. I've been

asked to model for a TV commercial, Dad, and some stills have to be taken today to show the advertising agency."

"Well, well." Carson Drew smiled proudly at his daughter. "That's wonderful, Nancy. What's the product to be advertised?"

"I haven't even asked yet," she giggled. "I'll probably find out today, and then I can tell you and Hannah all about it tonight."

When Nancy arrived at Rainbow Ranch and walked up the tree-lined, gravel drive, she saw four men standing talking near the stables. Some camera cases, tripods, and other equipment were piled nearby on the grass.

"Ah! Here comes our leading lady now!" Tony Traynor greeted her with a look of smiling approval. "Nancy, I'd like you to meet Marty Martin, my assistant." He indicated a slender young man with a shock of brown hair. "And this is Monsieur Philippe, our makeup artist."

The latter, a bearded man in his late twenties with a receding hairline, bowed and beamed at Nancy.

Tony examined Nancy's costume. "Your clothes should be just fine for these shots, Nancy. So if you'll just put yourself in Philippe's hands . . ." Turning to the makeup man, he said, "Take over."

Monsieur Philippe stepped forward, scrutinizing Nancy's features and hair. "There's not much I shall have to do," he announced judiciously. "A little more eye makeup and some highlighting of these wonderful cheekbones ought to do it."

With a few deft touches, shadowing the planes of Nancy's face, he achieved a surprising effect. Nancy scarcely recognized herself when he held up a mirror.

"What do you think, Tony?" Monsieur Philippe asked.

"She looks terrific to me!"

"Indeed, she does!" put in Roger Harlow, speaking for the first time. Up until that moment, he had remained silently in the background, letting the photographic specialists deal with the model for the commercial in their own way.

Nancy smiled back gratefully at the master of Rainbow Ranch. "We haven't even said hello yet," she greeted him.

"We'll chat later, Nancy."

At Tony's suggestion, they proceeded to the fenced-in paddock where a stablehand was waiting with a beautiful bay filly, saddled and ready for Nancy to mount.

"Oh, she's a beauty! What's her name?" the girl asked, patting the horse.

"This is Molly Malone. She never gives any trouble." The stablehand smiled and handed the reins to Nancy.

Tony Traynor and his assistant were busy preparing the cameras and using a light meter to check the intensity of the sunshine reflected from their subjects. Presently, as Nancy continued patting and talking to the horse, Tony began snapping pictures.

Without any trace of self-consciousness, she found herself responding easily to the orders and suggestions he called out.

As Nancy posed, she noticed a pretty little golden-haired girl some distance from the paddock. She was standing half-hidden by a tree, watching shyly as Nancy and the horse were photographed. She looked to be about seven years old and seemed ready to duck out of sight behind the tree at a moment's notice.

"Okay, Nancy, now mount up and ride around the paddock a couple of times," Tony called out. "Then come out of the gate and, let's see, ride across that brook on the far side of the drive and then circle back this way again."

Nancy obeyed, carrying out his instructions with the grace and poise she had acquired from performing in numerous horse shows. As Molly Malone

38

finally cantered out of the paddock, she noticed that the little girl had disappeared.

Nancy spurred her mount into a gallop as they approached the brook. She was pleased at the way the filly cleared the stream with an easy leap. As they circled through the trees beyond, a small, open pavilion came into view. The little blond girl was inside it, comfortably reclining on a wicker chaise, reading a book.

At the sound of approaching hoofbeats, the child looked up, her eyes widening in fear. With a scream of fright, she scrambled to her feet, her book flying to the floor of the pavilion.

Nancy reined up quickly and jumped down from the saddle, intending to apologize and reassure the little girl. But the child was already running off toward the house.

Disturbed by the incident, Nancy picked up the book, remounted, and resumed her ride. Tony was still snapping pictures swiftly as she came galloping up to the paddock, reined the horse to a halt, and swung down again from the saddle.

"Wonderful, Nancy!" Tony Traynor congratulated her. "I got some great shots! I think these should do it. I'll have them developed and show them to the agency tomorrow."

He turned and grinned as the owner of Rainbow

Ranch came walking toward them. "Well, how did you like our star?"

"She's every bit the horsewoman that you said she was!"

Roger Harlow smiled and patted the bay. "And how did you like this little filly, Nancy?"

"She's a lovely horse, Mr. Harlow." Nancy's face clouded as she went on, "But I'm afraid I accidentally frightened a little girl who was reading in the pavilion. I do hope she's all right! Here's her book."

"Thank you, Nancy. That was my granddaughter Tina, who's staying with me this summer."

As they strolled away from the paddock, Mr. Harlow went on, "I don't know what's gotten into the child. She was such a contented, outgoing little girl, but now she's so timid and unhappy she's even afraid of horses."

A sad look came over Roger Harlow's face. "Maybe she misses my wife. Tina loved her grandmother very much." He was silent for a moment, staring at the brook. "And then Tina's mother, my daughter Zona, had a bad fall from a horse soon after my wife's death. Perhaps all that was enough to cause the change in Tina."

Nancy said softly, "I'm so sorry, Mr. Harlow. I wish I could help. Is your daughter here?"

"No, she and Tina's father are taking a leisurely

40

cruise while she recovers from her accident. The odd thing is that, for the first week or two after Tina arrived, she seemed to be enjoying herself. Then she changed suddenly." The master of Rainbow Ranch shook his head. "I don't understand it."

As he finished speaking, a car came crunching up the gravel drive. It stopped near the stable where Tony Traynor had now joined Nancy and their host. A fair-haired man with a pencil-thin mustache stepped out from behind the wheel and waved to them.

"Hello, Hugh!" Mr. Harlow waved back.

"Uh—oh! Look who's here!" Tony muttered in an amused aside to Nancy. "That's Hugh Morston. He owns a New York ad agency that's been trying to snag the account we're doing this commercial for. I'll bet he came to find out what we're up to!"

As their visitor approached, Mr. Harlow said, "Nancy, I'd like you to meet Hugh Morston, my closest neighbor and fellow horse breeder. Hugh, this lovely young lady is Nancy Drew."

The newcomer flashed a wide smile. "Not related to Carson Drew, the lawyer, are you?"

Nancy smiled back. "Yes, I'm his daughter. Nice to meet you, Mr. Morston."

"And this is Tony Traynor," Harlow went on. "Or do you two know each other?"

41

"Yes, indeed," Morston replied as they exchanged cool smiles and a brusque handshake. "Well, Traynor, out here on business or pleasure? I heard you were shooting a commercial for Biddle and Downes."

"That's right. And this job's pure pleasure," Traynor said, smiling at Nancy.

"By the way, Roger," Hugh Morston said, turning to Mr. Harlow, "I don't like being the one to tell you, but I thought you ought to see a story in this morning's paper."

He took out the newspaper he was carrying tucked under one arm and handed it to Roger Harlow. It was folded open to the racing page. "I hope you'll publicly denounce this nonsense in the strongest possible terms!" he added, pointing to the article in question.

As Mr. Harlow read it, his expression darkened like a thundercloud. "This is outrageous!" he exclaimed, his face red with anger.

Suddenly, he clutched his chest as if struggling for breath. The next moment, he swayed and his legs seemed to give way beneath him!

5

The Surly Trainer

Tony Traynor moved swiftly to catch Mr. Harlow before he could fall. "Quick! Give me a hand!" he exclaimed to Hugh Morston.

Supporting the ranch owner under each arm, the two managed to get the limp and nearly unconscious man into the house. Nancy followed after picking up the newspaper that had fallen from Mr. Harlow's hands.

Once again, as on other occasions, her first-aid training proved invaluable. Nancy loosened her host's collar, had the two men elevate his feet, and then rubbed his wrists until Mr. Harlow's color began returning to normal.

Meanwhile, Tony Traynor had summoned the maid, who hastily brought her employer's usual medication. "He's supposed to take a spoonful of this twice a day," she said, her own face pale with alarm. "I remind him every morning, but often he won't bother."

With Tony's help, Nancy was able to spoon a dose of the medicine into Mr. Harlow's mouth, and presently he had recovered enough to sit up and talk.

"Shouldn't we call your doctor?" Nancy asked him anxiously.

"No, no, my dear. But I appreciate your concern." He patted her hand to reassure her. "It's my own fault for not following his orders. I suffer from a touch of high blood pressure, you see, but I'm quite all right now, thanks to you people!"

Hugh Morston apologized for upsetting his host with the unpleasant news item, although Nancy noticed that he did not really seem much disturbed by what had happened. He said good-bye and drove off a few minutes later. Tony Traynor also left as soon as he was satisfied that Mr. Harlow was all right.

By this time, Nancy had been able to glance at the newspaper. The item in question was a paragraph in a racing column:

Now that Shooting Star may not get a chance to run in the River Heights Handicap, many experts seem to be having second thoughts about the two-year-old's chances of winning that important race. Even his owner, Roger Harlow, is rumored to be worried that the stolen thoroughbred might not run well enough to justify all the money that was bet on him.

"Can you imagine how that makes me feel?" Mr. Harlow asked when he saw Nancy reading the column.

"Obviously pretty angry." Nancy hesitated before asking with a frown, "This implies that you won't mind if Shooting Star doesn't run in the handicap, doesn't it?"

"You bet it does! And that's not the worst of it. I don't mind telling you that I staked a lot of money on Shooting Star to win. But once the news came out that he'd been stolen, somebody began spreading a rumor that I'd staged the theft myself!"

"But why?" Nancy gasped incredulously.

"The rumor also hints that I knew Shooting Star wasn't in good racing form, and I didn't want to lose all the money I'd bet on him. Therefore I arranged to have him stolen so he wouldn't have to run. It's all untrue, of course. But now this columnist has spread the lie even wider by printing it in the newspaper!"

Nancy was shocked, but, in order not to raise her host's blood pressure again, thought it wisest to change the subject. "I guess that's all the more reason why we have to find Shooting Star as soon as possible," she said lightly.

"You're right, my dear," Roger Harlow agreed with a smile. "Suppose we go out to the stable now so you can see where and how the theft occurred."

Nancy reminded her host that perhaps he should not exert himself too soon after his attack, but Mr. Harlow assured her that he had entirely recovered and was feeling perfectly well.

Leaving the house, they strolled across the wide sweep of emerald lawn toward the white-painted, red-roofed stables. Like every other part of Rainbow Ranch, the latter appeared to be kept in very good order. Several horses could be seen grazing in the paddock, and at least one was being exercised by a groom.

After pausing on the way to point out each of his thoroughbreds by name, Mr. Harlow introduced Nancy to a man standing in the stable doorway who had been watching them approach.

"This is my trainer, Kurt Ellum," he said. "Kurt, this is Miss Nancy Drew. She's quite a sleuth. You may have heard of her. I'm hoping she can help us find Shooting Star."

The trainer gave a rather surly grunt. "She'll have to be pretty good to do that. Even the police don't seem to be having much luck."

Doffing his long-visored cap, he shook hands brusquely.

"How do you do," Nancy said with a smile. "You're right that it won't be easy to do better than the police. But I've worked with them before, and they always seem to appreciate any clues I can turn up."

Ellum, a heavy man with short, bristly, dark hair, was wearing a khaki shirt with rolled-up sleeves and jeans tucked into cowboy boots. "Lots of luck," he commented skeptically. "They've already been here a half-dozen times and questioned everyone who works around the stables."

Nancy refused to be put off by the trainer's rather scornful manner. His attitude seemed to imply that no mere slip of a girl had any chance of suc-

47

ceeding where regular officers of the law had failed.

After looking through the two connecting stable buildings, each one neatly partitioned into separate stalls, Nancy asked, "Was anyone on guard the night Shooting Star was stolen?"

"Yes, Alf Sanchez," Ellum replied bitterly. "He fell asleep on the job."

"Alf was a good enough stablehand," put in Mr. Harlow mildly. "I'm sure he didn't mean to let us down. But he's getting on in years and probably couldn't help dozing off."

Nancy noticed her host's use of the past tense in saying that Sanchez had been a good stablehand. "Doesn't he work here any more?" she asked.

"You think I'd keep him on after he let Mr. Harlow's best horse get stolen right under his nose?" Ellum retorted. "I fired him!"

"Where is he now?"

"I believe he's still living in Keanesville," said Mr. Harlow.

Nancy asked for his address and wrote it down, saying that she would like to question him.

"Go ahead," said Ellum, "but I can tell you right now what sort of silly story he'll tell you. He'll claim someone drugged his coffee thermos that night to make him pass out. That's the excuse he tried to hand us and the cops."

"Are you sure it's not true?"

"Absolutely! The police had his thermos tested in their crimelab and proved it contained no trace of any sleeping drug."

"It's understandable that Alf got drowsy," Roger Harlow put in. "As I say, he's an elderly chap, and at his age he needs his rest. It was no doubt my fault for not choosing one of the younger hands to act as watchman."

Nancy asked thoughtfully, "Could the noise of the fireworks be heard this far from the park?"

"Yes, that's a good point," Harlow said. "The cook was here, preparing a snack for us all when we got back from the celebration. She said the booms and bangs were so loud, they sounded as if the firecrackers were going off right outside the house. Undoubtedly, that's why the thieves picked that particular time for the theft—so the noise would cover any sounds that Shooting Star might make when he was taken from his stall. But once Alf got used to the sounds, they evidently weren't enough to stop him from dozing off."

Mr. Harlow invited Nancy to stay for lunch, but she explained that she had a date with her boyfriend. Ned Nickerson called for her soon after she returned home, and they started off in his car for a restaurant in River Heights.

"I saw Professor Barnes this morning," Ned reported. "He told me he called the contest sponsors, and they've agreed to let him change the information on the entry form. So now you can be listed as one of the actresses in our film and play the role we planned."

"Oh, Ned, I'm so glad!" Nancy said happily.

"Well, that's the good news."

"You mean there's bad news?"

"The worst! Because of that fire Saturday night, Ullman Realty has decided we can't use the Grimsby Mansion." The expression on Ned's face was as gloomy as his tone of voice.

"Oh, *no!*" Nancy exclaimed in dismay. "Surely, Mr. Ullman wouldn't be so unfair? The film club's not to blame for the fire!"

"He's convinced we *are* to blame, and the upshot is he's not going to risk any further damage to the property!"

Nancy fell silent as she pondered the problem. The realtor's attitude might be unfair, but there was no use complaining about it. The question was what could be done to change his mind? "I think we should ask Dr. Davis to talk to Mr. Ullman," Nancy declared after a few minutes. "She seemed like a very fair-minded person. Maybe he'll listen to her.

And I'll try to persuade him, too, Ned. Perhaps, when he calms down, he'll listen to reason."

"Thanks, Nancy. I hope you're right. But I sure wouldn't count on it!"

When they arrived at the Purple Parrot in River Heights, the restaurant was already filling up with noontime patrons and a cheerful buzz of conversation filled the air. Nancy was delighted to see her two closest friends among them.

"Look, Ned! There are Bess and George!" she murmured, waving.

Ned followed as she made her way to their table. Nancy hoped that Bess's and George's high-spirited chatter might help to cheer Ned up, and outwardly at least her plan seemed to work.

"Have you ever been to the Deene Art Gallery in Fernwood?" Bess asked. She babbled on enthusiastically when both Ned and Nancy shook their heads. "You should go. There's a marvelous exhibit of ceramics going on there. I'm dying to see it!"

"Guess why," George said jokingly. Then she confided to Ned and Nancy in an audible whisper, "A handsome sculptor's showing his work at that gallery. Bess saw his picture in the paper, so now she's trying every way she can think of to meet him!"

51

"That's not so, George! I really admire his work!" Bess declared, pink-faced with embarrassment. "Just because he's good-looking doesn't mean he can't be talented!"

"No, but it certainly helps to attract buyers," George retorted with a mischievous gleam in her eye.

"I suspect most artists do need encouragement before they become well-known," Nancy said. "I'll go with you, Bess."

"Thanks, Nancy," the girl said gratefully. "I'm sure you'll like this sculptor's ceramic figures as much as I do."

Ned seemed noticeably cheerful to Nancy by the time they said good-bye to Bess and George, but she was not prepared for what followed.

Ullman Realty was located only two blocks from the restaurant. As the two young people walked into the firm's storefront office, a woman receptionist frowned severely at them from behind her desk. The door to Mr. Ullman's private office was wide open. The realtor's face darkened with fury as he saw them. He sprang to his feet and burst from his office, shaking his fist at Ned.

"Get out of here this instant, you pyromaniac!"

6

A Crucial Test

Ned stood his ground and said politely, "Won't you at least give me a chance to—"

"A chance to what? Start another fire?" Ullman interrupted. "You and those other college kids have cost me enough already! The first day you're there, the stable burns down. A couple more days of your film shooting and I might not have any buildings left!"

"But we didn't start that fire."

The realtor gave an angry snort. "Huh! That's what *you* say!"

"It's true," Nancy said quietly but firmly. "Mr. Ullman, you have no basis for blaming what happened on Ned's film club."

"What do you mean?" The real-estate dealer, stocky and bald except for a fringe of graying black hair above his ears, turned to glare at the attractive teenager. "Wait a minute, aren't you Carson Drew's daughter Nancy? The amateur detective?"

"That's right." Nancy smiled back, relieved to see the realtor's irate expression relax a bit. "Mr. Ullman, Ned and I went to the dance at Westmoor University on Saturday night."

"I fail to see what that has to do with the fire."

"We passed the woods, both coming and going," Nancy told him. "On our way to the dance, there was no sign of any blaze. It wasn't until we were returning, sometime after eleven o'clock, that we glimpsed a red glow through the trees. And that was hours after the film club had left the mansion."

The realtor hesitated and frowned. "How do I know they didn't leave something smoldering?"

"But none of us smoke, sir," Ned cut in. "And we had no reason to light any matches."

"What time did you all leave?" Nancy asked Ned.

"A few minutes past five. I know because I went out last and locked up," he declared. "We were going to the dance so we had to get ready. We couldn't hang around."

Nancy turned back to the realtor. "Even if some-one *had* dropped a lighted match near the stable, it

54

certainly wouldn't have taken six hours for the building to catch fire! Whoever's responsible must have come around long after it got dark. That fact alone eliminates the members of the film club. I saw them at the dance myself."

"Well, I suppose if you can prove that . . ." Mr. Ullman's voice trailed off grudgingly. His manner no longer seemed so accusing.

Hoping to change his attitude even further, Nancy continued persuasively. "If you could just see your way clear to let us go on using the mansion, we'd not only do more cleaning up, we might even do some repair work. What do you think, Ned?"

"We certainly could," Ned agreed. "There are lots of loose boards that need nailing up, and we'd each be glad to throw in a full day of painting if the materials were supplied to us."

"Well, that seems fair enough," Ullman conceded, pursing his lips.

"Another thing," Nancy went on. "The name 'Ullman Realty Company' will appear among the credits at the end of the film. Isn't that so, Ned?"

"Of course! We were planning to do that automatically. It would give the firm some free advertising and also let the audience know who owns the Grimsby Mansion in case anyone seeing the film becomes interested in buying it."

It was obvious from the expression on his face that the realtor found this thought very appealing. "Very well. You may continue to use the mansion," he decided. "Provided you are very careful!"

The two young people happily thanked him and when they were outside, Ned gave Nancy a hug. "You're marvelous!" he told her. "Now we can get going on our film first thing tomorrow. And we'll work like a house afire!" Seeing the corners of Nancy's lips twitch, he added with a red-faced chuckle, "Oops, wrong expression!"

Ned had an afternoon class at Westmoor so he dropped Nancy at her home, where she quickly ran upstairs to get out of her riding clothes.

Feeling cooler in a simple yellow cotton dress, she called good-bye to Hannah Gruen and went out to her car. She was just about to slip behind the wheel when Bess Marvin came scampering up.

"A few seconds later and I'd have missed you," the blond girl said breathlessly. "Are you off to somewhere important?"

"I'm just on my way to interview someone about that stolen racehorse."

Bess's eyes widened. "You mean you're already on the trail of the crooks who did it?"

Nancy smiled. "Not exactly. The person I'm going to see is a stablehand named Alf Sanchez. He used to work at Rainbow Ranch, but he was fired for falling asleep on watch the night Shooting Star disappeared. Want to come along?"

"Wild horses couldn't keep me away!" Bess giggled as she got into the car.

They found Alf's house in a rundown section on the outskirts of River Heights. Some effort had been made to keep the place in repair, and Alf himself looked neat and cheerful even though he was evidently still out of work. He was smoking his pipe, rocking in a chair on the porch.

At the first mention of Shooting Star, Alf sat up straight, all attention. Taking his pipe from his mouth, he said, "Miss Drew, I was drugged. I don't care what anybody says. I was set to watch those horses that night and I was wide awake until I drank that coffee. When I'm paid to do something, I do it. I've never fallen asleep on any job in my life!"

Nancy said, "Mr. Sanchez, you know there was no trace of any drug found in the left-over coffee in the thermos, don't you?"

"Yes, at least that's what the police say, and that's why Kurt Ellum fired me. But then he always was a mean, suspicious sort. He'd have blamed me no matter what the report was from the police lab!" The former stablehand settled back in his chair again with a stubborn look on his face. Between puffs on his pipe, he added bitterly, "I worked at Rainbow Ranch a long time before Ellum ever came there."

"Well, if you think you were drugged, how do you think it happened?" Nancy leaned against the porch railing.

"I've been trying to figure that out, young lady, and it beats me." Sanchez frowned and shrugged his shoulders helplessly as he rocked back and forth. "I'll tell you one thing, though. That Shooting Star would have given whoever took him a lot of trouble! He's what you might call a horse with a mind of his own!" Sanchez laughed.

"Were you able to manage him, Mr. Sanchez?" Bess asked from the porch steps where she was sitting.

"Of course I could. I've been around horses all my life. There aren't any I can't handle. But don't go thinking that means I helped some dirty crook steal Shooting Star. I'd no more do a thing like that than I'd have let anyone hurt him!"

The former stablehand sounded so sincere that both girls were instinctively inclined to believe him.

"Mr. Sanchez, if you're telling the truth, perhaps

I can help clear you," Nancy said after a thoughtful pause.

The elderly man's face brightened hopefully.
"Miss Drew," he said, "from all I've heard and read
about you, you're a mighty smart girl. If you can
figure out how to prove I'm innocent, I'll sure be
grateful! Nobody will hire me again with this hanging over my head, and I'm just going crazy sitting
here day after day. I loved my job because I love
horses, and I've never done an injury to any horse or
any man in my life!"

Nancy promised to do her best to find some
evidence that would clear the former stablehand of
suspicion. As the two girls drove away, Bess said
anxiously, "Do you really think you can convince
the police he had nothing to do with Shooting Star's
disappearance?"

"I certainly intend to try," Nancy said in a
determined voice. "Facts are facts, and if Mr.
Sanchez is innocent, then the evidence should bear
him out."

To Bess's surprise, Nancy drove to police headquarters. In the building lobby, they were greeted
by a young red-haired policeman standing behind a
counter.

"Hello there, girls. Why, it's Nancy Drew! Just a

59

moment, let me ring Chief McGinnis. I imagine he's the person you've come to see."

"You're right. Thank you, Officer Worth." Nancy smiled.

A few minutes later, they were ushered into the office of her old friend, Police Chief McGinnis. "If it isn't two of my favorite people," he said smilingly as he rose from behind his desk to greet them. "What can I do for you?"

Nancy explained how the master of Rainbow Ranch had asked her to help in solving the mystery of his stolen racehorse. Then she added, "I was wondering if the thermos found next to Alf Sanchez that night is still in your lab?"

"Probably," the police chief said. "Let me check. Why? Would you like to examine it?"

"No, but I'd like your fingerprint expert to see if he can find any of Mr. Sanchez's prints on it."

After calling the crime laboratory and speaking briefly on the phone, McGinnis promised Nancy a report within twenty-four hours.

The Westmoor film club was to begin shooting their movie the following morning. Bess had expressed an eager interest in watching the filming so Nancy picked her up shortly before nine o'clock.

The day had dawned gloomy and gray with a

touch of fog, which forced the young driver to go slowly. Bess sat nervously peering through the windshield. She gave an explosive sigh of relief when Nancy stopped the car at the Grimsby Mansion.

"Ooh, it really does look spooky today, doesn't it?" Bess murmured, gazing at the old gray house in the swirling fog as they got out. "I wonder how the Grimsbys could stand to live here in the woods with no neighbors or telephone or anything."

"It does look brooding," Nancy agreed. "And it'll make a wonderful setting for the film. I wonder if Ned could get some outdoor shots in this weather just for atmosphere."

Just then the front door of the mansion creaked open, and Sara White smiled and called them in. "We're getting ready. Come on, Nancy. I'll show you where your gown is and where you can change. I'm to help you with your makeup."

The three girls trooped off upstairs.

"Tell me, Nancy, what's the plot of the film?" Bess asked excitedly as her friend was changing.

"Well, it takes place in old-fashioned times as you can tell from this gown. About the 1890s, I guess. And the heroine—yours truly," Nancy added with a smile, "has just moved into this mansion, which she inherited from her grandfather."

"Only she doesn't know the basement's inhabited by a creepy, old vampire!" Sara put in as she helped Nancy hook up the back of her gown.

Bess shivered deliciously. "Does he have designs on the heroine?"

"Of course! He falls madly in love with her!" Sara responded, getting out the makeup kit.

"Only he's terribly bashful," Nancy explained, "so he's afraid to come out in the open. He just keeps hovering in the background, scaring the wits out of everyone, including me!"

"He finally gets up nerve enough to come closer one evening when she dozes off on the sofa," Sara went on. "But remember, this vampire's about 500 years old. Just as he opens his mouth to sink his fangs into her lovely white throat, his false teeth drop out!"

All three girls burst into peals of laughter.

"Next morning, the maid sweeps them up," Nancy concluded between fits of hysterical giggling. "And the film ends the following night with the old vampire desperately picking through the trash heap, trying to find his fangs before sunrise!"

The scene that Ned and the group had decided to film that morning took place in the downstairs parlor where Nancy was entertaining an elderly doctor. He had come to warn her that spooky lights had been seen moving about inside the mansion late at night. During the conversation, Gwen, playing a maid, was to bring in a tray of refreshments.

The actors went through a brief rehearsal under Ned's direction. Then the lighting was carefully arranged and the shooting began. A girl named Jane Logan was operating the camera with Lenny Arthur acting as her assistant.

The scene began splendidly. But as Nancy chatted with the doctor, she noticed that one of the lights seemed to be moving. Apparently, it had not been clamped in position tightly enough, and Lenny went hastily to fix it.

The next moment, Nancy gasped and flung up her hand as the blinding spotlight shone right in her eyes!

"Lenny!" blurted a boy named Jack Billings, who was acting as electrician. "You've ruined the take!"

Gwen had just entered with the tray, on which were two glasses of fruit punch, and was approaching Nancy and the doctor as the lighting mishap occurred. In the resulting confusion, Gwen appeared to stumble and lose her balance, letting the glasses slip off the tray and spill the red liquid on Nancy's gown!

7

Silver Surprise

Bess, who was watching, cried out in dismay at the accident. But Nancy reacted quickly. She jumped to her feet and shook the liquid off the dress. "Give me some tissues, Bess!" she exclaimed.

By hasty wiping, the damage was soon repaired. "This fabric's so heavy, I don't think there was time for the punch to soak in," Nancy reported. "Anyhow, the skirt's too dark for any stain to show."

Ned tried to control his temper, but the strain of the urgent shooting schedule and the thought of the expensive, spoiled film made it hard not to show some irritation. "That was a dumb trick, Lenny!" he chided.

"Why blame me?" Lenny Arthur mumbled sullenly. "The light came loose, that's all. I tried to fix it, but it just happened to shine in her eyes for a second."

"If you'd clamped the light properly in the first place, it wouldn't have *come* loose!" Jack Billings flared back.

"Maybe the whole thing wasn't a dumb trick at all," Sara White said, staring coldly at Gwen Jethro. "I was watching you, Gwen. I think you tipped those glasses over on Nancy deliberately to ruin her gown!"

"Oh, don't be absurd!" Gwen tossed her head scornfully. "If Nancy hadn't made such a fuss over the light, all this wouldn't have happened. Everyone started talking at once and distracted me, so I didn't see where I was going. I just stumbled and spilled the glasses accidentally."

"Accidentally on purpose, you mean," Sara retorted in a dry voice laden with sarcasm.

Nancy couldn't help but notice that Gwen's eyes betrayed a gleam of mean satisfaction as if she were secretly enjoying the way Nancy's first scene had been spoiled. Nevertheless, the girl was anxious to smooth over any trouble that might disrupt the making of Ned's film.

"It really doesn't matter," Nancy interposed gently. "My dress wasn't ruined, so let's start all over."

Unfortunately, Gwen and Lenny were already much too disliked for the incident to be easily forgotten.

"This time, let's make sure all the lights are clamped good and tight before we start," said Jack with an exasperated glance at Lenny.

Mike Jordan had sponged off the carpet and was refilling the two glasses with fruit punch.

"Now, please watch where you're going, Gwen, so it won't happen again," Ned begged.

"You said it," Jane Logan cut in curtly. "We're not shooting this on a Hollywood budget, Gwen dear. In case no one's told you, film costs money and we don't have all that much!"

Her remark provoked an immediate retort from Gwen. Lenny Arthur, who was smarting from Jack Billings's caustic comments, joined in the exchange. Angry words were soon flying back and forth again as tempers rose. Both Ned and Nancy did their best to calm things down, but the quarrel had grown too bitter to be resolved.

In the end, Gwen and Lenny marched off together in a huff, slamming the front door of the mansion behind them.

There was a moment's silence before Ned sighed and shrugged his shoulders with a wan smile. "Well, do we quit right here or go on with our cinematic masterpiece?" he queried and looked around at the other club members.

"Of course we'll go on!" Sara White declared. "Who needs those two, anyway?"

There was a chorus of agreement.

"In that case," Ned suggested, "what about Bess Marvin taking Gwen's role as the maid?"

"Perfect!" Jack Billings exclaimed. Nancy had already noticed that he seemed to find her blond friend more than slightly attractive.

"How about it, Bess?" Jane Logan asked with a twinkle.

Pink-cheeked and thrilled at the unexpected invitation to act before a movie camera, Bess nervously accepted. Sara White, an expert seamstress, hastily let out Gwen's costume at the waist for Bess to try on. After a quick run-through, the scene was soon underway again, and to everyone's jubilation, the take was completed without a slip-up!

By noon, two more short scenes had been successfully filmed, after which everyone lunched happily on hamburgers and milkshakes that Mike Jordan brought from the nearest drive-in.

Ned and the other young men in the film club began to rearrange the furniture in the drawing room for the next scene. As Ned was pushing back a heavy armchair, a bright metal object caught his

67

eye. It turned out to be a slender, silver bud vase.

"Where'd that come from?" Jane asked in surprise.

"Under the chair. It must have rolled there and been forgotten some time or other, I guess."

"It feels heavy enough to be real silver, wouldn't you say, Nancy?"

"Definitely. Here's the hallmark." Holding the vase upside down, Nancy pointed to the maker's imprint stamped on the bottom.

"It looks like the Grimsbys' silver collection must be short one piece, then," Ned observed.

But the young detective shook her head. "I doubt it. All their valuables were cleared out years ago, and this vase certainly hasn't been here that long. The silver's still untarnished."

As she turned the vase over in her hand, Nancy's keen eyes noticed a slender monogram etched on one side. "Look! It's initialed with the letter W so it couldn't have belonged to the Grimsby family."

"Leave it to the super sleuth to spot all the clues!" Ned announced and grinned proudly. "If it didn't belong to the Grimsbys, how did it get under that chair, Nancy?"

"Good question," she replied thoughtfully. "I was wondering that myself."

The vase was put aside while the next scene was

being filmed. Afterwards, since their parts were over for that day's shooting schedule, Nancy and Bess said good-bye to the others and left. On a sudden impulse, Nancy took the silver vase with her, promising to turn it in to the police.

"Do you think it was stolen?" Bess asked as they drove off down the forest lane.

"There's one way to find out."

At police headquarters in River Heights, Nancy and her friend were admitted immediately to the office of Chief McGinnis.

"I'll have this checked out against our records of stolen articles," he said, setting the vase on his desk. "Thanks for bringing it in, Nancy."

"While I'm here," she said, "could you please tell us what your fingerprint expert found out about that coffee thermos?"

"Let's get his report right now. I'm curious, myself." Picking up the phone, the police chief spoke to someone in the detective bureau, and a few moments later a tall, dark-haired officer in plain clothes came into the office.

"This is Detective Hart, who's in charge of the racehorse case," McGinnis introduced him. "What did you get from that thermos, Phil?"

"Several smudged prints, Chief, none of them very good, but we'll check them out with the FBI.

One thing's certain, though. None of Alf Sanchez's prints are on the thermos. We know that for sure because we took his prints when he was first brought in for questioning."

Nancy was delighted at the news. "Then that can't possibly be his thermos!" she declared.

Detective Hart nodded. "I agree. If Sanchez had been drinking out of it that evening, his prints would have been all over it."

"So the thieves must have substituted a different thermos," she pointed out, "which means Mr. Sanchez's story that he was drugged may be true!"

Both Chief McGinnis and the detective agreed with the point. "I'd say it's almost certain he *was* drugged," Chief McGinnis added. "Otherwise, why would the thieves have bothered to substitute a different thermos? They were probably hoping we'd pin the crime on him, or at least concentrate our efforts on proving Sanchez was involved."

Detective Hart frowned and fingered his jaw thoughtfully. "There's another stablehand who's still under suspicion, though he claims to have an alibi."

"Who is that?" Nancy asked.

"Lou Yelvey. He used to work at Rainbow Ranch but was fired several months ago. If he's the type who holds a grudge, he might have given the thieves useful information about the stables, or he might even have helped them with the theft."

"That makes sense," Chief McGinnis remarked. "And if Shooting Star recognized Yelvey, that would have helped the crooks make their getaway without the horse kicking up too much of a disturbance."

Nancy considered this theory for a moment, then said, "Where is Yelvey working now?"

"He's out of work," replied the detective. "After Mr. Harlow fired him, he went to work as a stablehand for one of Harlow's neighbors, Hugh Morston. But he didn't last long there, either."

"You mentioned that he had an alibi," Nancy reminded him.

"Yes, he says he was out with a friend on the night of the theft. But we're checking every move they made to see if all their time is accounted for."

Detective Hart paused and gestured toward his superior. "The chief mentioned the thieves' getaway just now. Well, there's one odd thing about that. The theft happened on the Fourth of July, and there was lots of traffic on the road that evening due to people watching the fireworks. Yet we can't find a single witness who remembers seeing a horse trailer or a van that might have been used to carry off an animal of that size."

71

Nancy knit her brows. "That *is* strange."

Pointing to a wall map of the area, Hart continued, "So our theory is that Shooting Star may have been ridden all the way through Brookvale Forest. If so, the thief or thieves would have come out about here on North Road. That highway runs along the other side of the woods about two or three miles from Rainbow Ranch."

"You mean the crooks might have had some vehicle parked there to take the horse away in?"

"Right. As a matter of fact, we've already followed up on that possibility, and we've found several witnesses who say they saw a big black van parked there that evening just across from Tortoise Pond."

"Good work on that, Phil," Chief McGinnis commended the detective. Glancing at Nancy, he added, "The description of the van, by the way, matches one that was stolen over in Keanesville earlier on that same day. In the case of a big-time robbery like this, crooks often prefer to use a stolen vehicle, so if anyone spots it, there's no way it can be traced back to them."

Nancy thanked the officers for their information and left police headquarters with her girlfriend. Both were happy that Alf Sanchez appeared to be innocent.

"That was really smart of you, Nancy," Bess beamed as they got into the car, "to think of having the thermos checked for fingerprints."

The girl detective started the engine and steered smoothly into the stream of traffic. "Mr. Sanchez's innocence isn't the only thing this tells us," she confided.

"What else?" her blond companion asked in surprise.

"That the theft of Shooting Star was an inside job!"

8

Exciting News

"An inside job?" Bess echoed with a startled glance at Nancy. "You mean someone else at Rainbow Ranch may have helped the crooks steal Shooting Star?"

Her companion nodded. "Yes, I feel sure of it."

"But why? What makes you think so?"

"Because," Nancy replied, "if the original thermos of coffee was drugged, it was probably done by someone right there at the ranch. Most likely someone working either in the kitchen or in the stable. Or maybe by whomever brought the coffee out to Alf Sanchez from the house."

"You're right," Bess reflected. "It sounds so simple, and any of those people would have had the chance."

The girls were on their way to the Drews' house. The fog had cleared and a weak sun was shining through scattered clouds.

"Gosh, I hope Hannah has something good to nibble on. We've worked hard and I'm hungry," Nancy said.

Soon they were relaxing on the swing glider on the cool, screened-in side porch, with tall glasses of lemonade and a bowl of potato chips on a table in front of them.

But the quiet lasted only a few minutes. Then it was shattered by the shrill ringing of the telephone. Nancy jumped up. "I'd better answer that," she murmured. "Hannah's busy making a blueberry pie."

She returned shortly.

"Nancy, I can tell by the look on your face that you've had good news," Bess exclaimed. "Don't keep me guessing!"

"Yes, it was rather exciting," Nancy said and smiled. "That was Tony Traynor. He says the sponsor of that TV commercial I posed for has chosen me to do it. And, Bess, there are going to be three separate commercials!"

"Oh, super! Have you found out what product you'll be advertising?"

Nancy giggled. "Venus beauty soap!"

Her plump, blond friend grinned with delight. "Really?"

"Really what?" George Fayne asked as she came out on the porch from the living room followed by Hannah bringing the pitcher of lemonade and another glass.

"Nancy is going to do not one, not two, but *three* television commercials for Venus soap!"

"Why, Nancy, that's terrific!" George exulted. "You'll become even more famous!"

"She's right," Hannah said, smiling proudly at Nancy. She filled the glass she had brought with lemonade, then excused herself.

After chattering for a while, George and Bess left to do some errands. Nancy decided she had better tell Ned about her TV assignment. Perhaps together they could work out a schedule so that Nancy could be in the film and not hold up the club's progress.

"Hannah, I must drive over to Westmoor U to see Ned," Nancy said, bringing the empty glasses and pitcher out to the kitchen. "I'll be back in time for dinner."

Threading her way through the afternoon traffic,

Nancy had almost reached the university campus when she saw Lenny Arthur and Gwen Jethro in conversation with a spotty-faced young man standing by an open car door. He looked familiar, and from the way Gwen and Lenny kept casting furtive glances up and down the street, Nancy had the impression that they did not wish to be seen talking to him.

She puzzled over the young man's identity. Who was he and where had she seen him before? I'll ask Ned about him, she thought to herself. But by the time she found Ned in the film laboratory and they had discussed the problem of scheduling, the incident had slipped her mind completely.

Ned assured Nancy that the film club could easily shoot one or more scenes the next morning in which she would not be needed.

"I'm glad," Nancy said with a sigh of relief. "I was afraid I might hold things up."

As Ned walked her to her car, he asked, "Are you on your way home now?"

"No, I think I'll go over to Rainbow Ranch to see Mr. Harlow." Nancy had already told Ned how the ranch owner had asked her to help solve the mystery of his stolen thoroughbred. She related briefly how she had helped confirm the stablehand Alf Sanchez's story that he had been drugged.

A short time later, as Nancy turned up the tree-lined drive at Rainbow Ranch, she could see Roger Harlow walking back to the house from the stables. Parking her car, she hurried to join him.

A movement beyond the flowerbed on her left caught Nancy's eye. It was Tina kneeling on the grass and playing with a kitten. Nancy smiled and waved. The little girl stared at her, then quickly got up and ran off through the trees and out of sight around the other side of the house.

"Well, Nancy, what can I do for you?" Mr. Harlow asked with a smile as they met.

"I thought you'd like to know the good news about Alf Sanchez."

"Any good news will be welcome. Let's sit down on the patio and be comfortable while you tell me all about it." He led the way to some lawn chairs.

Nancy began, "Mr. Harlow, I thought a good place to start my investigation would be to check Alf Sanchez's story. So I asked the police crime lab to examine the thermos that was found by him."

"But they did," Mr. Harlow broke in.

"Yes, I know. And they found no trace of any drugs. But this time I asked them to test it for fingerprints. They did, and there were prints on it, all right. But none of them were Alf Sanchez's!"

As a startled look came over Mr. Harlow's face,

the young detective went on, "Don't you see? If he had drunk from that thermos, his prints should have been all over it. But they weren't. So the one that was found must have been substituted after he fell asleep, which means his own thermos could have been drugged, just as Alf says, but the thieves didn't want you or the police to know it so you'd think he was lying."

Mr. Harlow's face burst into a pleased smile. "By George, so he was telling the truth all along! I'm glad to hear it. That was mighty clever of you, Nancy!"

"Could you hire him back, Mr. Harlow?" Nancy asked hesitantly.

"My dear, that was my first thought. But I'm afraid it's not possible. You see, Kurt Ellum was the one who fired him, and I'm told he did it in a very harsh, unpleasant way. That's bound to leave bad feelings between them, so they could never work well together again. Also, Ellum is the trainer in charge of my stables, and if I hired Alf Sanchez back now, it might seem to the other hands that I was undercutting his authority."

He was interrupted by a maid bringing a tea tray out on the patio and setting it on a table between Nancy and Mr. Harlow.

"Thank you, Mary," he said. "Nancy, would you

pour and help yourself to these little sandwiches? I assure you they're too light to spoil your dinner, if that's why you're looking doubtful."

As Nancy smiled and filled a cup for him, he went on, "I'll tell you what I'll do. I'll give Alf a good reference, find him a new job, and see that he gets his full back pay."

"That will be lovely!" Nancy declared. As she bit into a delicious little cucumber sandwich, she went on more seriously, "But there's an unpleasant side to all this, too, Mr. Harlow. Do you realize that if Alf Sanchez *was* drugged, it must have been done by someone here at Rainbow Ranch?"

Roger Harlow's face darkened, and for a fleeting moment Nancy feared that he might be about to suffer another attack like the one she had witnessed on Monday morning. But his voice was quiet and steady. "I doubt that very much, Nancy," he replied. "No one here takes any sleeping pills or sedatives, so how could they have drugged Alf's coffee?"

Privately, Nancy wondered how her host could be so positive that none of his employees used such medication or had any in their possession. Perhaps his attitude was based on wishful thinking. Aloud, she said, "It would be helpful to know for sure. Do you think you could check and find out?"

"Of course," Mr. Harlow declared as he set down his teacup and reached for a small fruit pastry. "I just hope you can solve this case, Nancy, and discover what's happened to Shooting Star. We seem to be at a dead end."

Nancy smiled sympathetically. "Don't give up hope. There's something else I'd like to ask, Mr. Harlow. Do you have any enemy or enemies who might want to hurt you by stealing your best horse? Or is there anyone you suspect, no matter how illogical or improbable it may seem?"

Her host pondered in silence for several moments before replying. "I don't like to point the finger at anyone, you understand, but yes, there are four people who come to mind."

"Please tell me about them."

"Earlier this year, we had to fire a stablehand named Lou Yelvey. He was hard to get along with and caused a great deal of trouble in the stables just because he couldn't or wouldn't follow orders. When he was discharged, I'm sure he left with hard feelings."

Nancy remembered Yelvey's name as the suspect whom the police detective had mentioned earlier.

Mr. Harlow continued, "Then there was a jockey by the name of Pepper Nash. A year or so ago, he rode one of my horses in a race and totally disregarded his instructions on how to run it. I was angry and felt he had done it deliberately, so I accused him of throwing the race. Oh, not officially, mind you—it was just between us. But word got around, and pretty soon he couldn't get any horses to ride."

Nancy asked, "Do you know where Pepper Nash is now?"

"No. Shortly after that, he left town. I've no idea what happened to him." Roger paused unhappily. "I feel I'm getting pretty far out by mentioning these next two people. But anyhow, when I bought Shooting Star as a colt, I was up against a very eager rival bidder, a woman named Velma Deene. She owns an art gallery over in Fernwood." Seeing the expression on Nancy's face, Mr. Harlow broke off to inquire, "Do you know her?"

"A friend of mine happened to mention her art gallery, that's all. Please go on."

"Well, to make a long story short, I outbid her. Velma was very angry, especially since she and my daughter Zona had often been rivals at horse shows. Zona usually won, which made Velma quite bitter."

"I can imagine," Nancy commented. "It must have been very unpleasant. But you mentioned one more suspect."

"Yes, a sportsman named Judd Bruce." Again Mr. Harlow hesitated uncomfortably. "Judd has a horse entered in the River Heights Handicap. I'm certain that Shooting Star can beat him. So certain, in fact, that I've made a large bet with Bruce on the outcome. So you might say he has a motive for stealing Shooting Star. If my horse doesn't run, his horse probably can't be beaten and he won't have to worry about losing all that money he's wagered."

Glancing at her wristwatch, Nancy exclaimed, "I'd better leave, Mr. Harlow, or I'll be late for dinner! I'll check all those people out and keep you informed. Thank you for the delicious tea."

Her host rose and waved good-bye, then went indoors as she walked off down the drive. A moment later, Nancy stopped short, gaping at the windshield of her car.

There in blood-red crayon was a crude drawing of a horse alongside a skull and crossbones!

9

Hidden Names

Nancy stared at the sinister drawing on her windshield while a chilly feeling shot up her spine. Was this a warning not to get mixed up in the mystery of Shooting Star? A threat of harm if she tried to find the stolen racehorse?

Then another thought occurred to her. From the use of a crayon and the crude way in which the horse was drawn, it might have been done by a child. Could this possibly be Tina's work? Somehow, remembering the little girl's wide-eyed, frightened look, Nancy did not think so.

In any event, she decided just to drive off and say nothing about the drawing for fear of getting Tina in trouble. To create a fuss over the incident might only make it harder to make friends with the little girl if she were responsible for it.

Slipping behind the wheel, Nancy started her car and headed down the drive. Moments later, she pulled into the nearest service station to buy gasoline and have the red marks removed.

While the attendant was checking the oil and cleaning her windshield, Nancy pondered the mystery. Only one thing seemed certain. If Tina had not made the drawing, the crayoned threat was further proof that someone at Rainbow Ranch was involved in the theft of the racehorse.

As she paid the attendant and drove away, Nancy decided to visit Hugh Morston, whose estate was close to Rainbow Ranch.

Entering the beautifully landscaped grounds, Nancy saw the stables to the left of an ornate mansion. She could see Mr. Morston in a business suit talking to a groom in the stableyard. Morston's car was parked in front of the big house as if he had just arrived home.

Leaving her car there also, Nancy began walking toward the two men. Before she could reach them, however, Hugh Morston turned and started back toward his mansion. He smiled at the sight of her.

"Well, well, this is a pleasant surprise! Nice to see you. You've caught me just as I got home from New

York. I haven't even been in the house yet. What can I do for you?"

"Mr. Morston," she replied, "I'd like your opinion of Lou Yelvey. Did you know he's under suspicion of being mixed up in the theft of Shooting Star? The police are checking up on every move he made the night the horse was stolen."

Morston nodded and reached into his car to bring out a briefcase. Then he took Nancy by the elbow and began walking her up the broad marble steps to the door of the house. "Let's go in and have some refreshments while I answer your questions," he said, smiling at her.

When they were seated comfortably in the front room, sipping iced tea, Hugh Morston said, "I don't like to give anyone a bad name. I tried to help Yelvey out after he was fired from Rainbow Ranch, but," he said, shrugging, "the fellow was impossible. He was a troublemaker and very insolent. He just wouldn't take orders, so I had to let him go."

Taking a sip of the tea, Nancy asked Morston what he thought about the item in the newspaper that he had brought over to Rainbow Ranch to show Roger Harlow. "You recall what it said about Mr. Harlow doubting whether his horse could win the handicap. It implied that he himself might have had something to do with Shooting Star's disappearance. Do you really think he would do such a thing?"

Nancy settled back in the comfortable leather chair, curious to hear what her host would say. His answer surprised her.

"Well, it does seem fantastic at first thought, but, you know, a number of racing experts do believe that Judd Bruce's horse Minaret could beat Shooting Star."

Nancy remembered that Judd Bruce was the sportsman with whom Mr. Harlow had made his bet. He was also a possible suspect.

"Believe me, I have the highest regard for Roger Harlow," Morston went on. "On the other hand, horses and horseracing mean a great deal to him. He's spent his whole career breeding thoroughbreds. Who knows what anyone might do in a situation like that with an important prize at stake? Still," he smiled toothily at her, "what do I know? I'm only repeating what other people have been saying, my dear."

"Mr. Morston, I appreciate your honesty and also your willingness to answer my questions," Nancy said. "May I ask you one more?"

"Ask away, by all means."

"Do you remember a jockey named Pepper Nash?"

Hugh Morston thought for a moment, then nodded. "Yes, of course. I haven't seen him for ages. After word got around that Harlow thought he had deliberately lost a race, he couldn't get any horses to ride at tracks in this area."

Nancy asked, "Do you think the accusation was justified?"

"No. Nash was young and hotheaded. It was just poor judgment the way he handled his mount that caused him to lose. Of course, it was an important race for Harlow's horse, so it's understandable why Roger got so angry."

Hugh Morston politely walked Nancy to her car while chatting about the weather and his gardens. After saying good-bye and being assured that she was welcome at any time, Nancy drove off, wondering if Mr. Morston was as jovial as he seemed.

Heading into Fernwood, Nancy decided to call on Judd Bruce. His realty firm was on Main Street in a well-preserved, old colonial house, which had been very carefully restored. Inside, although the style of the rooms had been kept unchanged, it had been refurnished as business offices with all the latest equipment. Mr. Bruce was clearly prosperous.

Bruce himself was a stocky, balding man. His hearty manner turned to cold disdain when he discovered that Nancy was not a customer and learned the reason for her visit.

"I'm a busy man, Miss Drew," he said, looking at his watch. "I really don't know how you think I can help you." His hostile little eyes stared at her.

Nancy responded with a pleasant smile. "Mr. Bruce, as the owner of a valuable racehorse yourself, I was hoping you might have some thoughts about Shooting Star's theft. Perhaps you might even suggest some line of investigation to follow that hadn't occurred to me. For instance, what do you think of the rumor that Mr. Harlow was worried your horse could beat his?"

"Well, first of all, let me correct you when you speak of my horse beating Shooting Star. I am not the sole owner of Minaret. He is owned by a sporting syndicate of which I am a member."

Nancy was about to ask who the other investors in the syndicate were, when she noticed a sheet of stationery lying near the edge of Bruce's desk. The letterhead printed across the top said MINARET, INC. Underneath were several names, which Nancy could not make out. But she guessed that they must be the names of the various syndicate members.

Bruce saw what she was looking at, and his hand shot out, quickly turning over the piece of paper. "Secondly, for whatever my opinion may mean to you," he went on harshly, "if Shooting Star does run in the River Heights Handicap, Roger Harlow is going to lose a lot of money. Minaret will win. Does that answer your question?"

Judd Bruce stood up abruptly, ending the interview. He walked to the door of his office and held it open for her. "And now, Miss Drew, you'll have to excuse me."

How about that? Nancy mused as she walked to her car and drove away. Mr. Judd Bruce was a most unpleasant man. And so suspicious, too. He would certainly bear further investigation!

When Nancy arrived home, Hannah Gruen had just finished setting the table in the dining room and was lighting the candles.

"Hurry and wash your hands, Nancy. You're just in time," Hannah said.

"I'll be right there," the girl replied, racing upstairs.

She almost bumped into Carson Drew. "Whoa, honey! What's the rush?" the tall, distinguished lawyer chuckled, taking his daughter by the arms.

"Sorry, Dad, but Hannah said to hurry, and everything smells so good and I'm so hungry!" she smiled up at him.

He tilted her chin and looked at her fondly. "At the rate you're going, you'll beat me to the table!"

Later, over the delicious desert of chocolate mousse, Nancy told her father and Hannah of Judd Bruce's unfriendly attitude. "I'd like to know why he's so defensive," she added. "If he's one of a group of people who owns Minaret, why didn't he want me to see who the others were?"

"Good question," her father murmured as he sipped his coffee.

"Dad, is there any chance you could find that out for me? And also could your private investigators trace the whereabouts of a jockey named Pepper Nash? He used to race at tracks around here, but now he seems to have disappeared."

Carson Drew readily agreed to try to get the answers. "It may take a day or two, honey, but I'll let you know as soon as I learn anything."

The next morning dawned sunny and warm. Driving to the Rainbow Ranch to model for the first TV commercial, Nancy found Tony Traynor and his film crew already there. As soon as Monsieur Philippe had done his makeup work on her, she was ready to start.

A stable boy led a shining big black stallion out into the summer sun.

Tony said, "I thought Stormy would be a good horse to start with. Is it all right with you, Nancy?"

"Oh, yes! Isn't he a beauty!" She patted and soothed the restless animal.

"Okay, Stormy, here we go!" With that, Nancy lithely mounted him.

She was no sooner in the saddle than the big black thoroughbred began to buck and kick wildly. As he galloped and snorted, it was all Nancy could do to hang on!

10

Another Fright

Stormy continued to plunge and rear like an untamed bronco, calling on all of Nancy's riding skills to stay on his back. Seeing her chance, she jumped off quickly and at last was able to quiet the stallion.

"That was one time I was sure I'd be thrown!" she said to Tony Traynor and Kurt Ellum. The trainer had come hurrying to the scene, looking concerned during her wild ride.

Nancy continued patting and stroking Stormy to calm him.

"Here, let me take him! I'll get you another horse," Kurt Ellum said and reached for the reins in Nancy's hand.

"Too bad," Tony said regretfully. "He's a magnificent horse. Just what we need for this first commercial. You know, a different type of mount for each one."

"No, wait, please," Nancy said to Ellum, refusing to surrender the reins. "There must be a reason for him to act like that." Working deftly, she loosened the girth and pulled the light English saddle off Stormy. As she did so, a horse chestnut fell out from under the saddle and bounced on the ground.

"No wonder!" Tony Traynor exclaimed, picking up the prickly hulled nut.

"Stormy must have been in pain as soon as I mounted him," Nancy cried. "How did that ever get under his saddle?"

Kurt Ellum called angrily toward the stable, "Don!" Turning to Nancy and Tony, he said, "It's the fault of that fool stable boy. I'll fix him!"

When a long-haired boy of about fifteen came running out in response to Ellum's shout, he got a vicious tongue-lashing that left him close to tears. Nancy gently intervened, but he was marched back to the stable by Ellum with the horse walking between them.

In spite of having gotten off to a bad start, the shooting that morning went very well. Nancy rode and posed on a beautiful white Arabian horse named Snowflake, which Ellum personally brought out to them.

Afterward, Tony said, "I'd still like to shoot the next one with you on that black stallion, Nancy. Do you think you'd want to after this morning?"

"Indeed I would," Nancy declared. "It's bad for my morale to admit defeat. I'm going into the stable and talk to Stormy right now."

"Good luck!" Tony grinned. "The crew and I have to shove off. I'll see you here on Friday morning, okay?"

When Nancy emerged from the stable, Mr. Harlow was approaching. "I hoped I'd see you before you left, Nancy. I wanted to tell you that I've checked with all my employees. No one here at Rainbow Ranch uses sedatives or sleeping pills."

Nancy was still inclined to wonder how reliable his staff's answer to such a question might be, coming from their employer. But she replied politely, "Thanks for finding out. I guess I'll have to look elsewhere."

As they were talking, Nancy noticed Mr. Harlow's granddaughter walking slowly toward them. All through the morning's shooting, Tina had been sitting on a grassy mound across the brook, watching Nancy on Stormy and then on Snowflake. She had even responded with a little wave when Nancy smiled and waved to her.

When the little girl came up beside Mr. Harlow, he put his arm around her and said, "After that wonderful display of horsemanship this morning, I know Tina is eager to meet you. Isn't that right, dear?"

Tina smiled shyly and nodded. When Nancy smilingly offered her hand, the little girl took it.

Beaming, Mr. Harlow said, "Why don't we go back to the house and get the cook to rustle us up some refreshments? I don't know about you girls, but something cool would taste mighty good to me right now."

As they chatted on the patio, Nancy happened to mention that her boyfriend's film club was making an amateur movie not far from Rainbow Ranch. Tina looked so interested that Nancy asked if she would like to come and watch the filming.

"Oh, yes!" the little golden-haired girl exclaimed. "Can we go right now?"

"All right," Nancy smiled. "But first it might be a good idea to put on a pair of shoes or sandals, don't you think?"

Tina looked down at her bare feet and grinned. "I forgot. I'll be right back."

As she scampered off, Mr. Harlow looked gratefully at Nancy. "Bless you. I think your example on Stormy this morning may have put some fresh spirit into her. She was watching every minute, admiring the cool way you handled the situation."

"She probably just needs time to come out of her shell."

Roger Harlow sighed. "I hope so. She was such a happy, adventurous child when she first came this summer. She'd ride off on her pony and explore in all directions, even places like the Grimsby Mansion and that old mine down the road. When I found out what she was up to, I had to put a stop to it, of course. I explained that old deserted places like that may be dangerous. But I needn't have worried. Suddenly, she wouldn't go near her pony or stray very far from the house."

Concerned that she might be influencing Tina to disobey her grandfather's orders, Nancy promptly told him that the amateur movie was being filmed at the old Grimsby Mansion. "Would you rather she didn't go there?" Nancy asked.

"No, no! I'm delighted you've come up with something to catch her interest. I just felt it was risky for her to go poking around an old abandoned house by herself. But going there with you is different altogether," said Mr. Harlow.

When Tina came running up, he kissed her and

97

said, "Have a good time, honey! And, Nancy, you come back with Tina for lunch."

Nancy thought this might be an opportunity to help the little girl overcome her fear of horses. So as they left the house together, she steered the way gently toward the stables. "I think we can get there more quickly if we ride through the woods on horseback," she remarked casually.

Tina stopped abruptly with a look of alarm. "No, I don't want to!"

"Well then, suppose we just take one horse and ride double," Nancy suggested with a smile. "You can sit in front of me with my arms around you. How about that?"

But Tina shook her head stubbornly with an increasingly anxious expression. "No!"

"All right, dear." Nancy gave her small companion a reassuring hug. "We'll just walk, then. It isn't far."

"All right." Tina's face brightened at once. "Which way do we go?"

Nancy guided them to a trail through the woods, which led in the direction of the Grimsby Mansion. But as they strolled along the forest path, Tina's steps lagged. She began to walk slower and slower. Nancy noticed that the little girl's expression had become nervous and apprehensive.

"Is anything wrong, honey?" she inquired.

Tina shrugged and mumbled inaudibly.

Finally, as they came within sight of the house, Tina would go no further. Her face suddenly crumpled into tears. Turning, she began running back toward Rainbow Ranch, sobbing hysterically.

Nancy quickly caught up with the little girl. Rather than upset her with questions, she comforted and calmed her. Then they walked back, hand in hand, to Tina's grandfather's house. There they learned that Mr. Harlow had been called away to town on business.

So Nancy and Tina lunched alone together on the patio. As they enjoyed their sandwiches and milk and fruit, the two chatted lightly. Nothing more was said about the movie being filmed at the Grimsby Mansion or their walk through the woods.

Later, driving away from Rainbow Ranch, Nancy puzzled over Tina's strange behavior. What had caused the little girl's frightened outburst?

Before returning home, Nancy decided to talk to Lou Yelvey, the fired stablehand. Detective Hart had given her his address, which turned out to be a two-story house in the nearby town of Smithboro.

Nancy had just pulled up to the curb, when a thin, active-looking man came out of the house and started down the porch steps. In answer to Nancy's query, he grunted, "I'm Lou Yelvey. What do you want?"

The titian-haired girl explained why she had come and asked if he would mind answering a few questions.

"Go ahead," Yelvey shrugged. "But make it snappy. I've got a part-time delivery job now, and I'm due at the warehouse in twenty minutes."

"How did you come to lose your job at Rainbow Ranch?" she inquired, watching his face.

"I had a fight with Kurt Ellum, that's why. Look, I know horses, Miss Drew, and I don't need some bossy guy like him telling me all day long what to do and what not to do. We just didn't get along, that's all. As far as I'm concerned, he's a dumb cluck. And rotten-tempered, too."

Yelvey's jaw jutted out stubbornly as he spoke.

"What about your job at Mr. Morston's stables?" Nancy asked gently.

"You mean why was I fired there, too? You don't have to beat around the bush. I know the cops have got me on their little list of suspects! So what?" Lou Yelvey scowled and went on, "Look, I know I've got a short fuse. When I see something wrong, I speak out. That doesn't sit well with some people. Like Morston, for instance. That guy has no business owning horses. He doesn't know the first thing

100

about handling them! He's got a mean streak that comes out any time one of them acts up. When I told him so, he fired me."

Steering the conversation back to Rainbow Ranch, Nancy began asking him about the horses. To draw him out, she mentioned the ones that she had ridden. As Yelvey discussed them, Nancy could tell instinctively that he loved horses. While he might be quick-tempered and impatient with certain people, she sensed that he would be just the opposite with animals.

"What did you think of Shooting Star?" she asked.

"He's a fine horse with a great racing career ahead of him, if Harlow can ever get him back."

"Was he easy to handle?"

"Are you kidding? That horse has a mind of his own. Treat him right and he'll eat out of your hand. Otherwise he's apt to get ornery." Yelvey laughed. "You know, his best friend around that stable was a cat. It's a funny thing, but that cat would perch on the windowsill of his stall, and you'd almost believe they were talking to each other."

He added that he hoped Shooting Star would soon be found, and that if there was anything he could do to help, Nancy had only to ask. She offered him a lift to his delivery job, and they parted on friendly terms.

Returning home, Nancy quickly changed from her riding clothes. Since Hannah Gruen was out, she decided to pick up Bess and George and visit the Deene Art Gallery in Fernwood.

Bess was ecstatic. "Ooh, I'm just dying to see those ceramics! I loved the pictures I saw of them in the paper."

"Oh, sure. We know what really turned you on. It was the picture of the artist," George teased. "And he is handsome, I must admit."

Bess's cheeks were pink with excitement by time they arrived at the gallery. It was small but attractively arranged. The ceramics exhibit was set up in a corner of the main room. Several other people were examining the displays, and the girls had to move carefully among the stands and tables.

As Bess was examining the various pieces, a tall, severe-looking woman emerged from the back room. She wore her black hair parted in the middle and pulled tightly back into a bun at the nape of her neck.

Almost at once her glance lit on Nancy. With an angry gasp, she walked belligerently over to the girls with her hands on her hips and exclaimed to the young detective, "What are you doing here, you little snoop?"

Nancy was stunned. "What are you talking about?" she responded.

"Don't act coy with me. You know perfectly well what I'm talking about! You're Nancy Drew, aren't you?"

"Of course."

"I thought I recognized you! I saw your picture in the paper with a story about those television commercials you're appearing in out at Rainbow Ranch. And I suppose that underhanded sneak Roger Harlow sent you here to spy on me!"

Velma Deene's eyes flamed with rage at the very mention of her fancied long-time enemy. "He's probably even accused me of stealing Shooting Star. Well, you and your friends will have to leave my gallery this instant!"

Nancy realized that the woman was beyond reason. Turning to her friends, she murmured, "Let's go," and started toward the door in a dignified manner. George followed as coolly as Nancy. But Bess was in an agony of embarrassment. As she started after her two friends, she brushed against a piece of ceramic sculpture and knocked it over. It fell to the floor and smashed into tiny pieces!

11

A Painting Puzzle

The loud crash was followed by a dead silence. Bess went pale, then blushed crimson with shame. Everyone in the room seemed to be staring at her!

Her predicament became even worse as Velma Deene gave way to a fit of rage. "Just look what you've done!" she shrieked. "Ruined one of the prize pieces in the exhibit! How dare you teenagers come into my gallery and behave like rowdies!"

Sputtering with anger, the woman strode toward Bess, looking as if she were about to slap her.

Nancy remained calm despite the owner's display of bad temper. "There's no need to make a scene," she said in a quiet but clear voice. "We'll pay for the damage."

"I'll believe that when I see your parents walk in and hand me the money," Velma Deene retorted sarcastically. "In the meantime, you can clean up the pieces. Sheer vandalism, that's what it is. I knew you three spelled trouble the moment I laid eyes on you!"

This was too much for Nancy. "What was the price marked on that piece, Bess?" she cut in.

Bess groped nervously on the floor for the fragment of sculpture bearing a price sticker. "N-N-Ninety-nine dollars," she reported.

The gallery owner shot a withering glance at Nancy Drew as if to emphasize that this was far more money than any teenaged girl was likely to carry in her purse.

To the woman's surprise, Nancy took out her checkbook and a pen and coolly proceeded to write a check for ninety-nine dollars to the Deene Art Gallery.

"Good for you, Nancy!" George spoke up. "Bess and I will pay you our share as soon as we get home."

The other shoppers in the gallery had been watching in silence. But it soon became apparent from their expressions and their murmured comments that they sympathized with the three girls and thoroughly disapproved of the woman's harsh, insulting manner. One even turned and walked out with a look of disgust.

Seeing this, Velma Deene seemed to undergo a change of attitude. "Perhaps I overreacted a bit," she purred to the girls with a sudden, artificial smile, "but I've been through a very trying week, getting this exhibit organized."

As Nancy tried to hand her the check, she gushed, "No, no! You needn't pay for the figurine. I was forgetting all about the gallery's insurance policy. That covers any breakage."

The young detective would have insisted on paying, but Velma Deene brushed the check aside. So Nancy shrugged and put it in her purse, murmuring, "Whatever you say."

The spectators smiled and seemed almost ready to applaud as the three girls walked out. The owner, with a frozen smile on her face, was left to regain her poise and repair her shattered image in the eyes of her customers as best she could.

Outside, as the girls got into Nancy's car, Bess was tearfully apologetic over her clumsiness. "Oh, what an awful scene!" she quavered. "Breaking anything in a china shop or art gallery is bad enough, but a masterpiece like *that!* And then to have everyone stare at you with that woman carrying on the way she did!"

"Oh, forget it!" George said. "Nancy soon put her in her place."

"Even so," Bess said remorsefully, "I did break a ninety-nine-dollar ceramic sculpture!"

"Never mind, Bess." Nancy paused before starting her car to give her friend a comforting pat on the hand. "We'll make sure it's paid for one way or another."

She explained that Velma Deene was a possible suspect in the Shooting Star case, and that Roger Harlow had insisted on paying any expenses incurred in the investigation. "So I'll ask him to mail a check to the gallery, in case there's any problem with the insurance."

"Would you, Nancy?" Bess exclaimed, brightening gratefully. "I'll feel better knowing that, even though it doesn't make up for my clumsiness."

By the following morning, the girls had forgotten the unpleasant incident. Bess was not needed in any of the scenes of the vampire movie to be shot that day and had promised to go shopping with George, so Nancy drove to the Grimsby Mansion alone.

Bright sunshine was flooding down through the forest trees, and the old house looked almost cheerful with young people bustling in and out.

Nancy changed quickly into her costume and applied her makeup with a bit of help from Sara.

107

The first scene to be shot involved her and Mike Jordan, who was dressed in old-fashioned clothes to play her suitor. Nancy was supposed to be nervous over various spooky events that had happened the night before while Mike tried to soothe her fears.

Although he flubbed his lines on the first take, the scene was soon completed smoothly. Then everyone helped shift the lights and other equipment to the third floor. Here the script called for Nancy to discover strange footprints on the floor of an old room that supposedly had been kept locked.

"Move that light a bit closer, Jack, so we'll get some spookier-looking shadows," Ned suggested.

A sudden thud sounded on the stairway just below as if a foot had slipped on one of the steps.

Ned's eyebrows rose in surprise. "What was that?"

"Search me," said Jack. "We're all here, aren't we?"

There was a moment of silent counting. Everyone in the film club was either inside the room or hovering in the doorway.

Jane Logan seemed to finish counting first. "We must have a visitor!" she announced uneasily.

Her words were a signal for most of the group to run out into the hallway and down the stairs. Just as they reached the second floor, Ernie Gibson, who had played the role of the doctor on the first day of shooting, heard a sound from the corner room.

"In there!" he cried, pointing the way. Footsteps pounded in a rush to investigate.

Mike Jordan entered the room first. There was no one in sight, but he reached the open window just in time to glimpse a young man sliding down a back-porch roof to the ground. "There he goes!" Mike exclaimed.

As the others gathered around the window to peer out over his shoulder, two figures could be seen running off through the woods.

Another wild rush ensued, downstairs to the back door, in a frantic effort to nab or identify the figures. But as the club members emerged onto the back porch, they heard a car start up in the distance and speed away.

"What do you make of it, Nancy?" asked Sara.

"I've no idea. I never even got a look at them."

"I'll bet it was Lenny and Gwen," Jack said. "It would be just like those two to come back and try to cause some trouble."

But Ned shook his head doubtfully. "The intruders both looked male to me."

Nancy said nothing, but could not help thinking of the weird warning marked on the table top and the odd indications that Ned and Mr. Ullman had noticed of earlier visitors who had somehow gained entry to the mansion.

Rather than waste time dwelling on the incident, the group resumed filming. By early afternoon, an impressive amount of footage had been shot. "We're doing great," Ned congratulated the other members of the film club. "Keep this up and we may beat our own schedule!"

Turning to their movie heroine, he added, "And you're doing a terrific job of acting, Nancy!"

The others joined in with praise that made her blush.

Nancy's scenes were finished for the day. So after changing back to street clothes, the titian actress started happily out to her car.

As she walked through a room that led to the front hallway, Nancy paused. Almost without being aware of it, her trained eyes told her that something about the room seemed different. But what? In a subtle way, the sparse furnishings of the room had changed.

Puzzled, Nancy glanced over the few items of furniture but could not discover anything amiss. Then her gaze shifted to the walls, and suddenly she realized what had alerted her to attention.

A painting was gone!

12

Roadside Clue

For a moment, Nancy could not imagine what had happened to the framed picture. Nor could she recall exactly when she had last seen it.

But where had it gone? A break-in by burglars seemed unlikely. Yet none of the club members would have had any reason to take down the painting.

Nancy caught her breath as another thought suddenly struck her. *Those two intruders who had been chased away just before the second scene was shot!* Was it the painting they had been after? Yet, the slight noise that gave them away certainly had not come from this small downstairs room.

Nancy called Ned and the others. But none

of them could account for the missing picture.

"The question is, did those two snoops we saw take the painting?" Ned remarked.

"The one who slid off the roof certainly wasn't carrying anything," Mike Jordan declared.

Jack Billings looked at the puzzled group. "When we saw the two of them run off through the woods, they weren't carrying anything that big, either. At least, I don't *think* so."

The others agreed.

Nancy had been staring at the wall and thinking. "Look, people, we've been assuming all along that the picture was part of the old Grimsby furnishings."

"Sure, what else?" Mike said.

"But if that's so, how do you explain this?" Nancy pointed to the wall where the painting had hung.

"Explain what?" Sara asked in a puzzled voice.

Nancy said, "We know that the picture hanging there was square-cornered, don't we? But look at the wall stain."

The discoloration of the old tan wallpaper clearly showed the outline of an oval painting!

"You're absolutely right, Nancy!" Ned exclaimed. "If the picture that we saw had been up ever since the Grimsbys lived here, it would certainly have left its own mark."

"That's weird." Jane Logan shivered.

As the group broke up, they were still discussing the mystery. Nancy arranged to meet Ned at Westmoor University later, and then went out to her car. But she did not drive off immediately. She sat at the wheel for a while and mused.

The disappearance of the picture seemed baffling —as mysterious as the theft of Shooting Star. Who could have taken the painting? And why?

This certainly wasn't the first odd thing that had happened at Grimsby Mansion. Nancy was reminded of the silver bud vase that Ned had found. Like the missing picture, that also had not been part of the original furnishings of the old house, or so it seemed, judging by appearances. Were the two items connected somehow?

That last thought helped Nancy to decide her next plan. She would pay a visit to police headquarters to see if any information on the vase had turned up.

Nancy started her car and drove to River Heights. In the lobby of the police building, she encountered Detective Phil Hart.

"Sorry, Chief McGinnis isn't here," he told her with a smile. "He had to go see the dentist for a toothache. I have news for you, though, about that silver bud vase you brought in."

"Oh, yes." Nancy's eyes were bright with interest.

"That vase was reported stolen in one of those recent country-house burglaries. Remember the 'W' engraved on it? That was the detail that enabled us to identify it. The vase was reported stolen by the owners, named Waggoner, on May 9th."

Nancy pondered this information for a moment, then said, "I have some news for you, too, Detective Hart." She told him about the missing painting and added, "It showed a hunting scene with hounds and red-coated riders. I noticed it particularly because one of the horses in the picture reminded me of my own horse, Black Prince. Do you suppose that painting might also have been stolen just like the silver bud vase?"

"Let's check it out," the detective said. "Have you got a few minutes, Nancy?"

"Yes, of course."

He took her up by elevator to the second floor. When they were both seated in his small office, he took a sheaf of papers from his desk drawer and skimmed through them.

"Ah, here's the list," he said presently. A moment later, as he ran his finger down the page, his eyebrows suddenly rose. "Well, well, well! Here's a

114

painting that was reported stolen on June 21st in another of those country-house burglaries. It's described as a nineteenth-century hunting scene in a gilded frame measuring approximately thirty-six inches by forty-eight inches, with scarlet-coated huntsmen riding with hounds."

"That's it!" the girl cried excitedly. "I'm sure of it!"

The detective beamed at her. "Nice going, Nancy. It looks like you've given us another lead on these robberies."

Nancy smiled regretfully. "A lead maybe, but not the painting itself, unfortunately. Do you have any clue as to who's committing those country-house burglaries?"

"Not really. The roads around that Brookvale Forest area where the crimes have occurred are all well patrolled at night. Yet the burglar's only been seen once and even then he was disguised!"

Detective Hart related that one of the robbery victims had been awakened one night by a noise in his living room and had come downstairs in time to surprise the robber snatching an expensive clock off the mantel. The thief had on a black Halloween costume with a white skeleton painted on both the front and the back, and a skull mask to match.

"That doesn't give you much to go on," Nancy murmured sympathetically.

The police detective grinned back at her. "Don't worry. It just takes patience. Give us time and a few breaks, plus some more help from Nancy Drew, and we'll nab him yet!"

An hour later at Westmoor University, Nancy met Ned as he emerged from the film lab. She quickly told him the news about the silver vase he had found and the painting taken from the Grimsby Mansion. The boy was startled.

"Why on earth would the robber dump part of his loot *there*?" he puzzled. "Such an out-of-the-way place as an old house in the woods. It's like the middle of nowhere!"

"I agree it doesn't seem to make much sense," Nancy said. "The obvious thing would be to take it to the nearest big city, where he could find a professional fence to help dispose of the stolen goods. But he must have had a reason."

She mused in silence for a moment, then looked up at Ned with a smile. "How would you like to drive out to North Road with me right now?"

"What for?"

"A black van was seen there on the night that Shooting Star was stolen. The police think that may be how the horse was carried off, so I'd like to

116

search for clues." With a twinkle, Nancy finished, "It won't be out of your way because I'm inviting you to dinner tonight. Hannah's making a shrimp casserole and I know you love that."

"Uh—oh!" Ned laughed. "You just said the magic word. I'll come peaceably."

Driving along North Road, which bordered Brookvale Forest, Nancy located Tortoise Pond with no difficulty. Witnesses had said the van was parked just across the road from the pond.

Nancy and Ned searched for clues in the tall grass bordering the road. With a sudden cry, she swooped down on a broken piece of fan belt.

"Look at this, Ned," she said. "Could this have come off the van?"

"Maybe." He inspected the object closely. "But even if it did, this wouldn't be enough to help you identify the make or model, if that's what you're thinking."

"Not exactly." There was a thoughtful frown on Nancy's face. "Suppose this did come off the van. Would that disable it in any way?"

Ned shrugged. "It might. That depends on how many belts the van's engine had, and which one this was. If the crooks didn't know it was gone, the van might have overheated and stalled before they'd driven very far."

Nancy was excited by his answer. "If that did happen, Ned, the thieves would have been in a mess! Just imagine being stranded out on the road late at night with a stolen racehorse in their van. They might have had to abandon the van and escape on horseback!"

Ned chuckled. "That sounds like a Wild West movie! But assuming you're right, what do we do now?"

"Simple. Let's drive along the road and look for an abandoned van."

"We don't even know which way they went."

"So we'll try both directions," Nancy said with a smile. "Let's try away from River Heights first."

"Sounds reasonable," Ned agreed.

A few moments later, they were driving slowly along the highway. Less than two miles from Tortoise Pond, Nancy suddenly stopped and pointed. "Look, Ned! I think I see it!"

13

Smoke Scare

Ned stared in the direction Nancy was pointing. The reddish rays of the setting sun shone right in their eyes, silhouetting the treetops and leaving the trunks and underbrush in gloom. But he could make out the shape of a large black object half-hidden among the trees.

"You're right!" he exclaimed suddenly. They both got out of the car and hurried to investigate more closely. It was, indeed, a black van.

"Good thinking, Nancy," Ned said, giving her a quick hug. "This has got to be the one the police are looking for."

"Let's check and see if the fan belt is missing," Nancy said.

119

Ned lifted the hood and confirmed this fact. There were also rust stains on the engine and the front of the van as though the radiator had boiled over. This further bore out Nancy's theory, which had led to the discovery of the abandoned vehicle. Apparently, the driver had turned off onto the shoulder of the road and then plowed through the underbrush to a spot well in among the trees, where the van would not be too noticeable to passing motorists.

"If we hadn't come along this way looking for it, Nancy, I'll bet the van could have sat here for months!" Ned declared.

Nancy glanced into the driver's compartment. "Look," she said, opening the door to show Ned. "The crooks didn't even bother taking the keys. They're still in the dash."

"If the van was stolen, they probably didn't care." As he spoke, Ned started around to the rear of the vehicle, intending to look in back. But the door handle would not turn.

"That's strange," Nancy murmured.

"What is?"

"They would have had to open up this loading door, wouldn't they, to let the horse out after they got stuck here?"

120

"Sure." Ned looked puzzled. "But so what?"

"They didn't lock the front doors. They even left the keys behind. So why bother locking this door?"

"Hmmm, that is odd now that you mention it." Suddenly, a startled look came over Ned's face. "Good night! You don't suppose Shooting Star is still in there?"

"I hope not, for his sake!"

Ned hastily got the keys from the ignition and unlocked the back of the van. As the doors swung open, he and Nancy stared in combined relief and surprise. The inside of the van was filled with tools and old, discarded auto parts. Used tires and mufflers, old batteries, rusted bumpers, and hubcaps were strewn carelessly about or stacked in piles. It looked like a junk shop on wheels. Certainly, no horse could have been in this van on the night of the Fourth of July!

"What do you make of it, Nancy?" Ned asked with a puzzled frown.

"I'm not quite sure but I'm beginning to have a deep-down suspicion," she replied, dimpling mischievously.

Going back to her own car, Nancy took a notepad and pen from her purse, then wrote down the van's make and license number. "Let's lock it up and call the police, Ned."

Her friend hesitated. "Shouldn't we take the keys to the police station so they can send someone out here and get the van moving again as soon as possible? Those tools in there are valuable, especially to their owner."

"You're right, of course," Nancy agreed. "Come on. It's a little out of our way, but it won't make us late for Hannah's dinner."

When they stopped at police headquarters, both Chief McGinnis and Detective Hart were out. The young people left the keys and information about the van with one of the officers on duty and drove on to Nancy's house.

The Drews, Hannah Gruen, and Ned were just finishing their dinner when the phone rang in the hall.

"I'll get it," Nancy said, jumping up. "It's probably Bess." But she was wrong.

As she walked thoughtfully back into the dining room a few minutes later, three pairs of eyes were fastened on Nancy's face.

"That was Chief McGinnis," she reported, "with news of that black van Ned and I were telling you about. He said that its license number matched that of the van stolen from Keanesville just hours before

Shooting Star disappeared. Undoubtedly, it's the van that was seen parked on the edge of the woods the night of the theft."

"Nancy, I still don't get it." Ned frowned. "We know that it was never used to carry a horse, so why should we assume that it had anything at all to do with the theft?"

"Because in my opinion it was used to mislead the police," Nancy replied with a twinkle. "In other words, that black van was just a red herring all along."

"You mean they never intended to use it for transporting Shooting Star?"

"That's right. I believe they just wanted the police to *think* that's how the thoroughbred was taken away."

"By George, that would certainly fit the facts," Carson Drew remarked thoughtfully.

Ned slapped the table and exclaimed, "If you're right, Nancy, that means Shooting Star may still be somewhere in this area!"

"Exactly," Nancy said and nodded.

The next morning, she arose earlier than usual. She was due to meet Tony Traynor and his crew for the next TV commercial to be shot at Rainbow Ranch. While dressing, Nancy decided that she would have enough time to drive to the stable where she kept Black Prince and ride him to Mr. Harlow's estate. Prince needs the exercise, she reflected, and it will give me a chance to show him to Tina. The little girl had been quite curious when Nancy told her all about him.

When the young detective arrived at Rainbow Ranch, Tony and his assistants had just gotten there. Stormy, the black stallion, had not yet been saddled and brought out of the stable.

Seeing Black Prince, Tony immediately recalled the episode that had first given him the idea of using the sleek thoroughbred's attractive rider in the commercial. "That horse of yours is a beauty, Nancy! Would you mind if we used him instead of Stormy?"

"Of course not," Nancy said. "If we do, everything will go very smoothly, just wait and see!"

And indeed, after Monsieur Philippe had finished making her up, everything went off with perfect precision. Nancy and Black Prince worked so beautifully together that Tony was amazed.

"That's a wrap," he declared, using the expression for a satisfactory take. "We've got all that we need!"

He and his crew started to pack up, still marveling at how quickly they had finished shooting. Just before climbing into his car, Tony called out, "I'd like to do that last commercial Monday morning, Nancy. Can you make it?"

"I sure can," she replied with a smile.

"And this time it'll be a horse of another color!" Tony drove off laughing.

Before she left, Nancy coaxed Tina into patting Black Prince and even feeding him a lump of sugar. Then she and the little girl strolled along the brook to a point where it widened into a pool. As they chatted, Nancy noticed a tortoise-shell cat on the other side of the pool. She was gazing down into the water intently, perhaps watching minnows.

Tina saw the cat, too. When Nancy asked if she belonged to her, Tina said, "Oh, that's Patches. She's not a house cat. She lives in the stables. But she's fun to play with!"

The pretty little creature seemed familiar, somehow, and suddenly Nancy realized where she had seen her before. Patches was the cat that had startled Bess's horse when the three girls were riding through the woods on the previous Saturday.

When Nancy arrived home and changed out of her riding clothes, she and Hannah sat down to a quiet lunch of quiche and a green salad. Later, as they were finishing dessert, Nancy put down her napkin with a sudden gasp of dismay.

"Oh, Hannah, I shouldn't have taken so long over

lunch. Come on. I'll help you with the dishes and then I must go to the Grimsby Mansion. I almost forgot. Ned and the film club are shooting this afternoon!"

She was about to start clearing the table when Hannah stopped her. "Nonsense, dear. These few dishes won't take long. You go ahead so you won't be late." The motherly housekeeper was very insistent, so Nancy reluctantly left.

When she arrived at the old mansion, she found the club members starting to unload their equipment and set it up inside. The last group pulled up in a car just as the girl was stepping out of hers.

"Hi, Nancy! All ready to emote?" Jack Billings grinned.

"Emoting's the word, all right," Sara White chimed in with a smile at Nancy. "We're going to shoot that scary scene where you—"

She was interrupted by a sudden yell from Mike Jordan. "Hey, look up there!"

All eyes turned upward. Anxious gasps and exclamations followed immediately. Smoke was pouring from an upper-floor window on one side of the house!

"Oh, no!" Ned groaned. "Not another fire!"

Within seconds, it seemed, black clouds of smoke

were billowing high above the treetops. Yet there was no sign of flames.

"No telephone!" Ernie Gibson exclaimed. "One of us had better go call in an alarm!"

Ned dashed toward his car, but before he had time to start the engine, fire sirens could be heard screaming in the distance.

"It sounds like the smoke's already been seen," said Mike.

Springing into action, Nancy exclaimed, "But there are still no flames, and the smoke's only coming from one window! I'm going up and have a look!"

Over protests and warning cries from the others, she ran into the house and started upstairs. Ned and several others followed.

Reaching the third floor, Nancy could still see no sign of a fire, nor, as she cautiously touched the door to the room, could she feel any heat. Through the haze, she saw that the fumes seemed to be issuing from an object on the floor.

"I believe it's a smoke bomb!" Nancy cried.

Just then, they heard a fire truck rumble up outside the house, and soon the fire fighters came dashing up the stairs. Ordering the film group aside, they opened the door and saw the bomb.

"All right, what's the idea of playing such a prank? Haven't you kids got anything better to do than fool around causing trouble?"

Nancy realized that if any such suspicions got back to Ullman Realty, the mansion might be closed to the film club permanently. Thinking quickly, she turned to Ned. "When was that window opened?"

"Just before lunch," he replied. "This place smelled so musty, I wanted to air it out a bit before we started shooting this afternoon."

"Well then, it must have happened during lunchtime." Turning back to the fire chief, she pointed out the window and said, "Someone must have climbed up that tree and tossed the bomb in while no one was here. We certainly wouldn't have planted it just to make trouble for ourselves. Surely you can see that."

One of the firemen spoke up to his chief, "She could be right, Bert. This bomb has a delayed-action timer on it."

The tree in question was growing so close to the house that its thick branches could easily be reached from the window. Ned climbed out on one of them to examine the trunk. Presently, he called, "Hey, people, look at this!"

As the firemen and club members crowded around the open window, Ned pointed to fresh scratches on the tree bark. Then he bent his head and peered closely at something among the leaves. "And here's a piece of evidence that the bomber left behind!" he exclaimed. "It snagged on one of the twigs!"

With a triumphant grin, he plucked it loose and held up a bit of greenish fabric!

14

Ghostly Hecklers

Ned's discovery seemed to convince the firemen that no one in the film club had planted the smoke bomb as a prank. The piece of greenish fabric was the final proof.

"You can see for yourself, Chief," Ned said as he climbed back in through the window and held out the material. "None of us is wearing any clothing of this color."

"You've made your point," the fire chief conceded. "It looks like the young lady was right. Some outsider must have climbed the tree and tossed in the bomb."

"Maybe it's the same troublemaker who burned down the stable," another fire fighter remarked.

The fire truck finally rumbled off with its crew, and the college group went ahead with their filming. Nancy and the other actors played their parts dramatically, and the spooky scene, after only a single flub and retake, was soon completed to everyone's satisfaction.

The next scene did not go quite as well. Ernie Gibson had trouble with his lines, causing Ned to break off filming long enough to make some hasty changes in the script. His rewrite of the scene played so effectively that the onlookers broke into spontaneous applause as soon as the action ended and Ned shouted "Cut!"

"That was great, everyone!" he added as the applause tapered off.

A third scene was also shot successfully that afternoon. It, too, drew cheers and applause. Nancy went off, flushed and happy, to remove her makeup and change back to street clothes, while the club members packed up their equipment.

Ned was waiting for her in the front room of the mansion as she came down the curving staircase. "Do you think you could come back tonight?" he asked. "I'd like to shoot one of the outdoor scenes."

She agreed enthusiastically. "Conditions should be perfect. A clear sky and a full moon!"

"Just one thing," Ned warned, suddenly looking

grave and worried. "Watch out for werewolves and vampires!"

He broke into an eerie, wolf howl that left Nancy giggling helplessly.

"Come to think of it, I'd better pick you up," Ned said. "Is seven too early?"

"No, fine! I'll try to be ready."

On her way home, Nancy decided to stop off at the River Heights Public Library. Why don't I read up on racing, she mused. It might give me some ideas that would help to unravel the Shooting Star case. Although she already knew a good deal about thoroughbreds from her show riding, Nancy realized that she had much to learn about the sport of horseracing and the business of bloodstock breeding.

She parked her car and walked into the library. The reading room was moderately full of people for this late hour of the afternoon. Nancy went first to the card catalog and looked in one of the file drawers under HORSES to find the location of her subject.

Moments later, as she closed the drawer and started toward the reference shelves, her gaze fell on a familiar figure. That's Hugh Morston, Nancy thought. He was standing at the magazine desk on one side of the room, evidently asking for a back issue of some periodical.

As the librarian came out of the stack room and handed him a magazine, Morston thanked her and turned away. Nancy would have said hello as their paths converged. But he sat down at a table without speaking and leafed open the magazine. I guess he didn't see me, Nancy told herself.

She found a whole shelf full of books on horses, dealing with every aspect of the subject, from riding and caring for horses to racing and breeding. There were also colorful volumes showing the many breeds found throughout the world.

Nancy picked out two books that looked particularly interesting and started toward the checkout counter located near the door. As she emerged from between the shelves, she saw that Hugh Morston was no longer seated at the table reading. But the magazine still lay open where he had left it.

Nancy glanced at the periodical in passing and saw that it was a copy of a well-known news magazine called *World*. A strangely familiar face on the left page caught her eye, yet she could not quite place it.

Suddenly, Nancy caught her breath. That's Roger Harlow! she realized. What had kept her from recognizing him at once was the fact that he looked considerably younger in the picture than the man she knew now.

Pausing for a closer look, Nancy read the caption. It confirmed that the person in the photograph was Roger Harlow. From the date on the cover, she saw that the magazine was ten years old.

Obviously, Hugh Morston had been looking up an old story about his neighbor. But why? And what exactly did it say? Intrigued, Nancy sat down to scan the article.

The story, which was in the business section of the magazine, told of a bitter fight between Harlow and an industrialist named Howard Ainslee for control of a large corporation. Apparently, the struggle had gone on for months at a cost of millions of dollars.

Nancy closed the magazine with a troubled sigh, then picked up her books and carried them to the checkout counter.

When she arrived home, her father put down the evening paper to greet her with a kiss. "How goes the vampire movie, dear?"

"Great so far, Dad! It may not win the contest, but I think Ned and the film club will at least end up with a good entry."

"Tell us all about it at dinner, dear," Hannah Gruen called from the dining room. "The chops are almost ready."

Nancy quickly freshened up and joined the others as they were about to sit down at the table. "Mmm, these biscuits looks yummy enough to melt in my mouth, Hannah!" she exclaimed.

Carson Drew and the housekeeper listened with interest as she described the afternoon's filming and told of the smoke-bomb scare.

Later, over dessert, Nancy changed the subject. "Dad, do you remember a business hassle ten years ago involving Roger Harlow? He and a man named Howard Ainslee were fighting for control of a company called the Ludex Corporation."

"Yes, vaguely. Why do you ask?" When Nancy explained, Mr. Drew said, "As I recall, the company was having financial problems. Harlow and Ainslee were both trying to take it over. They got into what's called a proxy fight, each one trying to buy up enough stock to gain control. It was a long, drawn-out struggle. Harlow finally won, but I'm afraid in doing so he made a bitter enemy of Ainslee."

The lawyer paused to stir and sip his coffee. "Speaking of business, Nancy, you were asking me before about the syndicate that owns that racehorse Minaret."

"Oh, yes, Dad! Were you able to find out anything?"

"A little. It's a three-man syndicate. Judd Bruce

acts as front man for the other two partners. One of them owns only ten percent. But the other is the biggest investor of the three and owns more than fifty percent."

"Who is he?" Nancy inquired keenly.

Carson Drew shrugged and shook his head. "That I can't tell, my dear. In fact, I'm not even sure it's a man. The names of the syndicate investors are not on public record. What I've just told you I found out from some of my legal contacts in the racing profession."

Their conversation was interrupted by the mellow toll of the door chimes.

"Oh, dear, it's later than I thought!" Nancy exclaimed and jumped up from the table. "That must be Ned now."

Her guess was right, and the two were soon on their way to Brookvale Forest in Ned's car. The velvety, dark-blue sky was studded with stars, and a round orange moon glimmered down through the trees as they turned up the wooded lane that led to Grimsby Mansion.

"What a perfect night for a vampire scene!" Nancy said enthusiastically.

"You're right," Ned agreed, turning to glance at her and reaching out for her hand. "Almost too perfect to waste shooting a movie!"

Nancy smiled and gave him a quick kiss on the cheek.

Lights were glowing from the windows of the old house, and most of the film club members were already on hand as Nancy and Ned drew up in front. The place was soon bustling with activity.

In the scene to be filmed, Nancy, her fiancé, and the elderly doctor were to rush out of the mansion with a lantern after glimpsing a weird face peering in at them. At first, they would only see a bat fluttering among the trees.

Then the script called for Nancy, who had wandered off a little way from the others, to notice a figure beckoning to her just beyond the aura of light from the mansion's windows. Mistaking the figure for that of her fiancé, she would run toward it, only to find herself face to face with the vampire!

Ned—marvelously made up with slicked-back hair, a black cape, and fangs—was to play the vampire. There was a brief run-through of the action, and the lights were carefully arranged. Then the filming of the scene began.

The club members held their breath in suspense. Everything seemed to be going perfectly! Jane Logan kept the camera trained on Nancy as she started toward the beckoning figure.

Suddenly, a flash of light blazed out from among

the trees, bathing the night in dazzling brilliance! Nancy stopped short in confusion, almost blinded by the flash.

Angry shouts and groans arose from the club members. "Who would pull a trick like that?" Jack Billings demanded indignantly.

"Maybe the same two jokers who spied on us yesterday," Mike Jordan suggested. He and the other young men darted to hunt for the perpetrators. They soon gave up, however, realizing that it was hopeless in the darkness.

Ned was as angry as the others, but felt they should go on filming. "Maybe we can salvage most of the footage."

"What if those nuts do the same thing all over again and spoil another take?" Sara asked anxiously.

Ned gave a helpless shrug. "We'll just have to take our chances, I guess. Otherwise we may as well give up for the night."

Once again, filming got underway with Jack holding out a mike on a boom and Jane Logan operating the camera. Nancy resumed her actions from the point at which the scene had been interrupted.

But as she ran toward the beckoning figure with an eager cry, loud mocking voices blared out from the woods all around them!

15

Spook Trap

The scene was ruined, and the club members were furious.

"Let's get those rats!" Jack Billings exclaimed.

"We'll need more light than this," Ned warned. "We haven't much hope of finding them in the dark."

Hastily snatching up what flashlights were available, the whole group spread out into the woods, hoping to catch at least one of their tormentors. No lurking figures showed up in their flashlight beams. Every now and then another taunting voice would jeer at them from the darkness. But always, it seemed just out of reach.

Ned heaved an angry sigh of frustration. "Oh,

what's the use? This game of hide-and-seek could go on all night!"

Nancy said, "Wait, Ned! Shhh!" The two had just made a mad rush to a spot where a voice seemed to be coming from, but had found no one.

They had a single flashlight between them. Only leafy underbrush and the tree trunks all around them were visible in its glow.

"Did you hear something?" Ned asked, lowering his voice.

"No, but I'm sure we made no mistake about the direction of that voice we heard," Nancy replied with a puzzled frown. "There must be someone or something concealed around here, Ned!"

They stood silently for a while, listening. Ned swung his flashlight beam here and there, probing the darkness. Their wait seemed useless, and they were just about to move on when a shrill voice came from the shrubbery at their side.

Whirling, Ned aimed his light into the foliage.

"Look!" Nancy gasped.

There, hidden among the leaves, was a walkie-talkie radio propped among the branches of the shrubbery! Another loud jeer blared from the device as they stood looking at it.

"No wonder we couldn't catch anyone," Ned said angrily, reaching for the walkie-talkie.

"Wait, don't move it!" Nancy said urgently. "I've a plan." Looking around, she added, "Ned, could we remember this spot well enough to find it again?"

"Sure, I guess so. But why?"

"Come on, let's get the others! I'll tell you on the way." As they headed back toward the house, Nancy went on, "Where do you suppose whoever's doing this is broadcasting from?"

"Who knows? Probably somewhere in the woods close enough to see us. But they could be a mile away. It all depends on how powerful their sets are."

"So we might be wasting our time searching around here," Nancy pointed out.

The two stopped near the mansion and called out to the others. Ned also waved his flashlight to catch their attention. Singly and in pairs, the rest of the club came walking back empty-handed and frustrated. Ned told them what he and Nancy had found.

"Ooh, I'd like to get my hands on those wise guys," Mike said. "I'd teach them a lesson!"

Nancy said, "They've been clever. But we'll fool them. Let's pack up our equipment and drive away."

"You mean just give up?" Denise said. Other voices were raised in protest and disbelief.

141

"I don't mean leave for good," Nancy explained. "I just mean drive far enough away to make them *think* we've gone for the night."

She pointed out that walkie-talkie sets were expensive, and that the hoaxers must have placed several around the mansion. "Surely, they won't go off and leave them," Nancy reasoned. "So we'll sneak back on foot and catch them red-handed when they come to collect their sets."

The film club greeted her plan with a show of enthusiasm. They packed away their equipment and turned off all the lights in the mansion. Then Ned locked up the place. Piling into their cars, they deliberately slammed the doors noisily and started the engines with a roar, hoping to be heard by the hoaxers. But they drove only to the edge of the forest, where the entrance lane branched off from the North Road.

Parking quietly out of sight by the roadside, they took their flashlights and hurried stealthily back to the mansion.

"Spread out!" Ned hissed to the others. "And try not to be seen!"

He and Nancy retraced their steps toward the spot where they had found the walkie-talkie and crouched down in a clump of underbrush nearby.

Several minutes passed. Nothing was heard except the gentle sighing of tree branches in the evening breeze, the occasional call of a night bird, and the chirping of crickets. But presently, footsteps were approaching through the woods.

"Here they come!" Nancy whispered, clutching Ned's arm.

A voice spoke in the darkness. "All clear?"

"Sure, the house is dark," another voice said. "They've gone."

"Okay, the fun's over, I guess." A third speaker chuckled. "Let's get our walkie-talkies and leave. I bet we really had 'em tearing their hair!"

In a moment, a darkened figure appeared through the trees, coming toward the spot where Ned and Nancy were hiding. He switched on a flashlight and shone it down among the shrubbery, looking for his walkie-talkie. As he bent down to pick up his set, Ned sprang out of the underbrush and grabbed him in one swift movement!

"Hey!" the searcher blurted in a terrified voice. But instead of releasing him, Ned twisted his arm behind his back so he could not get away.

Nancy shone the light on his face. It was the spotty-faced youth that she had seen talking to Gwen Jethro and Lenny Arthur on the street near Westmoor University.

"Ned," Nancy cried, "he's from Burnside Tech! I

remember him from the dance. He's in their film club!"

Meanwhile, the two other Burnside Tech students had been caught by the rest of the Westmoor group. One of them sheepishly admitted that he had been the intruder who slid down the porch roof. The spotty-faced youth, whose name was Cliff, had been with him.

"Gwen and Lenny told us what your film was about," Cliff confessed, "so we decided to find out if it was as good as it sounded."

"And maybe keep us from finishing it before the deadline!" Jack Billings cut in belligerently.

The Burnside trio did not try to deny the charge. But they insisted that they knew nothing about the missing painting, the smoke bomb, or the fire. "We'd never do anything like that, honestly!" the apparent ringleader declared. "We just wanted to pester you enough to hold up your shooting schedule."

Nancy was inclined to believe him, as were most of the Westmoor group. "But," Ned said, "that's not all you fellows did. We not only lost time due to your dirty tricks; we also wasted a lot of expensive film footage!"

"How about if we replace the wasted film?" Cliff said guiltily.

"And promise not to pull any more funny business," the ringleader added. "Will that square things?"

The Westmoor club members agreed that they would be satisfied with these truce terms, so the Burnside trio was allowed to leave with no worse punishment than the derisive grins and jibes of their erstwhile victims.

After getting their cars and setting up their equipment once more, the film club resumed shooting. It was almost eleven o'clock before they were through, but by that time the night scene had been filmed successfully and everyone was happy with the results.

"We're still going to have to work double time though, to bring this in under the wire!" Ned told them.

The next day, Nancy put on jeans and a cotton print shirt and left early for the Grimsby Mansion. As she drove past Hugh Morston's opulent estate, she saw him on the lawn, examining a big evergreen tree. On impulse, Nancy stopped and greeted him.

"Well, Nancy," Hugh Morston said and smiled, "to what do I owe the pleasure of this visit?"

Nancy related how she had seen him at the library on the previous evening, reading a magazine, and how the sight of Roger Harlow's photograph on the open page had caused her to stop and skim the article about his feud with Howard Ainslee.

"Forgive me if I seem snoopy," she went on, "but do you mind telling me why you looked up that article?"

Morston seemed shaken by her question. "Just curiosity, I suppose," he said with an awkward shrug.

"Why now? Did you know Howard Ainslee?"

"I didn't at the time of his trouble with Roger Harlow, but I've met him since." Mr. Morston seemed reluctant to say anything further, adding, "I really know nothing about the matter, beyond what we've both read."

But Nancy persisted. Smiling winningly at him, she said, "Mr. Morston, if you know anything at all that might possibly have a bearing on the Shooting Star case, it would be such a big help."

Hugh Morston's troubled expression relaxed and the corners of his mouth twitched slightly. "Nancy, you could charm the birds out of the trees, I'm sure," he said.

With a sigh, he went on, "Well, there's just one thing I can tell you. Ainslee recently moved into this area. Less than a month ago, he bought a house on the other side of Brookvale Forest."

146

16

A Shimmer of Beauty

Nancy was startled by the news about Roger Harlow's old enemy, Howard Ainslee. If Ainslee now lived in this area, he might well be involved in the mystery that she had been asked to solve!

"Thank you, Mr. Morston," she said slowly. "You've certainly given me something to think about."

Her informant stroked his thin mustache and shrugged. "Just a small piece of information, my dear. It may or may not be important. That's for you to judge. If there's any other way I can help, please call on me."

"I shall. And thanks again, Mr. Morston."

As she drove off, Nancy pondered what she had

147

just learned. Was it possible that Ainslee still bore a bitter enough grudge against Roger Harlow to have stolen his prize thoroughbred? The idea seemed fantastic, especially after a lapse of ten years. Yet both men had invested millions of dollars in their feud with the result that Ainslee had lost his chance to win control of a vast corporation. Surely, crimes had been committed in revenge for far lesser grievances than that!

For that matter, maybe Howard Ainslee was still trying to take over the same company and felt that any trouble for Roger Harlow would work out to his own advantage.

Nancy put the whole matter out of her head as she parked her car in the courtyard of the old Grimsby Mansion. Most of the Westmoor film club members had already arrived and were busy getting set up to begin shooting.

Denise Foley came scurrying up eagerly in a full-skirted gown as Nancy entered the house. "Do I look all right in this silly bonnet?" she asked a trifle breathlessly.

Nancy could see that she was nervous at the prospect of acting in front of a movie camera with the rest of the film club looking on. "Of course! It's perfect!" she assured Denise.

The first scene that morning was to be filmed in

the parlor. Denise was to play the role of an inquisitive neighbor. She had seen a tall dark stranger in a black cape lurking near the mansion at twilight the previous evening, so she was calling to find out if Nancy had attracted a new suitor.

The filming began soon after Nancy had changed into her costume and applied her makeup. All went smoothly as Ned called "Cut!" and ordered spotlights to be moved into position so the two actresses could be photographed in close-up.

"Hey, what's that?" Mike muttered suddenly. He held up his hand, signaling the others to be still for a moment.

A sound could be heard coming up through the floor!

"It sounds like something ringing down in the basement," said Ned. He looked around at the other club members. "Is anyone down there?"

Heads were shaken. "No, we're all here," Sara White replied.

Although nobody said so, everyone immediately wondered if another intrusion was taking place.

"I'd better go see," Ned said.

"We'll both go," Mike declared.

The two young men started down the hallway leading to the rear of the house. The others followed uneasily. But when Ned pressed the switch for the

149

landing light, the back stairway remained dark. Nor could any glow be seen from below when he pressed the cellar light switch.

"That's funny," Jack Billings said with a frown. "They should both work. We replaced every bulb in the house."

"Never mind. We can grope our way down," said Ned. "There's probably enough light coming through the basement windows to see what's ringing."

"No, wait!" Nancy spoke up anxiously. "Those stairs are too steep to take any chances!"

She dashed out to her car and returned with a flashlight. "Here, use this!"

Ned grinned and flicked it on. "Whatever you say, ma'am." He started down the steps with Mike close behind him.

They had just gone around the bend of the landing when the others heard startled exclamations from the two youths.

"What's wrong, you guys?" Jack called.

"Take a look!"

As the others crowded down the stairs and craned for a glimpse, they saw that a wire had been stretched at ankle height across the third step down from the landing!

"Good grief!" Jane Logan gasped in dismay. "You

two could have fallen and broken your necks!"

Ned Nickerson nodded grimly. "We would have if Nancy hadn't insisted on me taking this flashlight!"

The ringing noise could still be heard, although it now seemed to be dying away. While Mike disconnected the wire, Ned went on down to investigate. He soon returned to the foot of the stairs to show the others what had caused the sound.

"An alarm clock!" Sara exclaimed. "Whose is it?"

"Good question," Ned responded. "Will the owner please speak up?"

Nobody said a word.

"The next question," said Ned, "is why the lights won't work." He went off to check the fuse box. Presently, he called out. "Try turning them on now!"

When Jack pressed the switches at the top of the stairs, both the landing and basement lights went on.

"The fuses were unscrewed," Ned reported.

Nancy was horrified. It seemed clear that someone had deliberately set a booby trap for them. The alarm clock must have been placed in the basement the night before and set to go off the following morning. And the same party had no doubt stretched the wire across the stairs and unscrewed the two fuses. As a result, anyone who went down the unlit steps to investigate the alarm sound was almost certain to trip over the wire!

"I'm still not sure what's going on," Nancy confided to Ned a little later when they were alone for a few moments. "But whatever it is, this is more serious than we realized."

Ned nodded, his face grave. "I agree. I wonder how the creep who set the trap got into the house last night."

"Are there any signs of a break-in?"

"The door locks haven't been tampered with. I've already checked. Of course, whoever did it might have pried open a window, I suppose."

Despite the ominous way in which the day had begun, two good scenes were successfully filmed during the morning. As lunchtime approached, Ned mentioned to Nancy that Bess Marvin would be needed again that afternoon to play the role of maid.

"I know. I phoned yesterday to remind her," Nancy said. "In fact, I promised to go and pick her up."

Bess was ready and waiting when Nancy arrived at the Marvins' house. The plump, blond girl was bubbling over with excitement, eager to resume her movie-acting career.

"What happens today?" she asked, settling herself beside Nancy in the car.

"Oh, a couple of juicy scenes. One of them," Nancy added with a giggle, "is where you accidentally sweep up the vampire's fangs!"

After stopping on the way for hamburgers, they drove to the Grimsby Mansion. Nancy was not needed for the sweeping scene so she did not get back into costume immediately. She was opening the drapes wider in the sitting room in order to provide more light for the filming, when her eye was caught by a glimmer of colors from the bushes just outside the window.

"Oh, my goodness! What's that?" Nancy said. She hurried outside for a better look and returned moments later, wide-eyed at her discovery.

"What is it?" asked Bess, who had just come downstairs in her maid's costume. She gasped as Nancy showed her what she had found. "An *opal!*"

"And it's *huge!*" Denise said as she and the other club members crowded around to see it.

The lovely gem was aflame with color and attached to a silver chain.

"How on earth do you suppose it got out on that bush, Nancy?" asked Sara.

The titian-haired sleuth shook her head. "I've no idea. But I'm sure I know whose it is. I've seen it in a portrait of Mr. Harlow's late wife at Rainbow Ranch!"

There was no time to return the pendant that evening as Nancy had a Saturday night date with Ned. But the following morning, she drove to Rainbow Ranch. As she got out of her car, Tina came skipping up.

"Hi, Nancy! Did you come over to play with me?"

"Well, that's partly why I came," Nancy said and smiled. "But I'm also bringing something back to your grandfather."

Tina's face blanched in terror as she saw the opal. "No, please!" the little girl begged. "You *mustn't*!"

17

Tina's Secret

Nancy was astonished and disturbed. What had come over the child to upset her so dreadfully?

Tina, meanwhile, was watching the teenager's expression with almost tearful anxiety. "What are you going to do, Nancy?" she asked, clasping and unclasping her hands distractedly.

Nancy said gently, "I found this in the shrubbery at Grimsby Mansion, and I thought I recognized it. Isn't this the opal pendant that your grandma wore in the painting?"

"Yes, oh yes, it's Grandma's! But what are you going to do with it?" Tina persisted fearfully.

"Return it, of course. Surely, that's the right thing to do, isn't it, if you find something that belongs to someone else?"

But the little girl only trembled and choked back sobs as she struggled to express herself. "Nancy," she gulped, "would you please give it to me so I can take it upstairs right now and put it back in the drawer where it belongs?" Tina's voice broke with emotion. "And would you please, please not say anything to Grandpa about it? Oh, please!" she begged with tears in her eyes.

Nancy hesitated uncertainly. "Tina," she pleaded, "can't you tell me why you're so upset?" As the little girl shook her head, Nancy went on, "Then can't you at least tell me how the opal got to Grimsby Mansion?"

Tina gave another vigorous shake of her head, her golden locks swinging from side to side.

"Where is your grandpa, honey?" Nancy asked after a moment.

"In the library talking on the phone. But *please* don't tell him, Nancy!"

Suddenly, the detective came to a decision. Handing the opal pendant to Tina, she said, "All right, dear. You go on upstairs and put this away right now."

The little girl's tearful expression gave way to a grateful smile. Without another word, she turned and scampered off with the necklace.

Did I do the right thing? Nancy wondered. Oh

dear! I just hope this may help me win Tina's trust and confidence.

She was just walking to her car as the little girl came running out of the house again.

"Oh, don't go!" Tina seized Nancy's hand. "I want to thank you."

"Maybe someday you'll be able to trust me enough to tell me about it."

Tina nodded solemnly, looking much calmer now.

"I have to go," Nancy said with a smile. "But I'll be back tomorrow morning to do the last TV commercial. See you then, dear." She waved goodbye.

As she was driving home, Nancy remembered that Hannah Gruen had asked her to bring back some shampoo. So she stopped at a drugstore in town and went in. While she was looking over the various brands on the shelves, trying to find the one Hannah preferred, Nancy heard a faintly familiar voice raised in protest.

"I tell you I *must* have this refilled! It isn't as though I didn't have a prescription."

Looking up, she saw a tall, black-haired woman standing at the drug counter. As the woman went on speaking in a fretful, demanding fashion, she was interrupted by the patient voice of the pharmacist.

"I'm really sorry, ma'am, but I'm only allowed to give you one refill on this prescription, and you've used that. What I can do is call your doctor and see if he'll allow another refill—although it may take me some time to get through to him. It often does, if they're busy seeing patients."

"Hmm, very well," the customer agreed grudgingly. "I certainly hope you can do something. I've been having such trouble sleeping these last few nights! I'll drop in later to pick it up."

As she turned away toward the door, Nancy recognized her with a slight start. The woman was Velma Deene!

A sudden thought struck the youth sleuth. Was it possible that some of the woman's sleeping pills had been used by the thief to sedate Alf Sanchez on the night that Shooting Star was stolen?

Velma Deene walked out without noticing Nancy, who purchased the bottle of shampoo she had chosen and left the store.

Soon after the Drews had finished a quiet Sunday dinner, Bess, George, and then Ned dropped over. They listened to records for a while and chatted. Then Nancy brought them up to date on the Shooting Star mystery, including her morning glimpse of Velma Deene. In doing so, she mentioned the fleeting thought that had passed through her mind.

"It wouldn't surprise me a bit to find out she was mixed up in something like that," George declared. "If you ask me, that woman's capable of anything!"

"She's certainly very unpleasant," Bess said. "I think it's strange that someone like her should be running an art gallery."

"Why, Bess?" Ned asked, smiling.

"Well, people who appreciate beauty are more sensitive than her type, I think." Bess added shyly. But that's just a personal feeling."

That evening Hannah Gruen went off to visit a friend, while Nancy and her father spent the time catching up on their reading.

On Monday morning, Nancy awoke with a sense of excitement. Not only was this the day for shooting the last TV commercial, but she had a feeling that something significant was going to happen.

Nancy laughed at herself as she set out for Rainbow Ranch. Whatever happens, let's hope it's good, and not something like my car breaking down! she thought.

Tina was waiting for her as she drove up and parked. The little girl seemed in high spirits. She took Nancy's hand and chattered, "Those TV people just came a little while ago. Mr. Traynor's chosen the horse that you're going to be on. It's Firebird. She's my mother's horse, and she's *so* beautiful! She's trained to do just about everything. I bet Mr. Traynor chose Firebird because she's red and your hair is, too!"

Nancy chuckled. "Perhaps so, dear. I'd better go join them. Are you coming?"

Tina shook her head. "I'm going over to sit by the brook where I usually do." And she ran off.

On her way to the stables, Nancy met Roger Harlow. After greeting him, she said, "Tina tells me I'm to ride your daughter's horse this morning. I hope that's all right."

"Of course, it is," he said and laughed. "She'd be glad to have someone like you take Firebird out every day. Has Tina gone inside?"

"No, she's over there by the brook, all set to watch the filming."

Mr. Harlow said earnestly, "Nancy, she's almost her old self again, and I know I have you to thank for it. I'm very grateful!"

Nancy smiled at him. "I'm glad if I've been able to help a little."

As she walked away, however, Nancy reflected that Tina evidently still didn't trust her enough to confide in her.

Tony was especially pleased with the filming that morning. "Nancy, with you on that beautiful red horse—well, it just makes a stunning picture!" He shook his head. "I don't know how you did it, but each new commercial seems to turn out better than the last one!"

The crew quickly packed up and prepared to return to New York in his station wagon. Tony turned to his model with a parting remark. "Young lady, if you ever decide you'd like a career in this field, just give me a call and it's yours!"

Nancy smiled and thanked him warmly. "It's kind of you to say so, but I don't think that's where my real interests lie. If I ever change my mind, though, I'll remember what you said."

She waved as the TV group drove off. Afterwards, Nancy continued to ride Firebird for a while since the filly seemed to enjoy the exercise. Finally she dismounted and walked the beautiful horse to the stables where she turned her over to a groom.

Coming out, she found Tina waiting for her, obviously seeking her company. The little girl was bouncing a large, orange-and-yellow-striped beach ball. "Would you like to play catch with me?" she asked shyly.

"Oh yes, I'd love to, dear," Nancy replied.

They crossed the brook, heading toward a hilly

161

meadow with plenty of room in which to play. Tina was very agile, and the game got wilder and wilder. She dashed about with her golden hair flying.

Finally, in running after the ball, which had gotten past her, Tina stumbled and lost her footing. The next moment, she was tumbling down a rough slope toward a marshy pond!

18

Suspect's Return

Just in time, Tina grabbed hold of some bushes and saved herself from falling into the pond.

"Are you all right?" Nancy called out, running to her assistance.

"Y-Y-Yes, I think so."

Thankfully, Nancy helped her up the slope. Except for some scratches and a slight tear in her shirt, the little girl seemed unharmed.

Nancy gave her a reassuring hug. "Do they hurt much?" she said, looking at the scratches.

Tina shook her head and gave a little grin.

"Let's get over to the stables and attend to those, shall we?" Nancy had noticed a well-stocked, first-aid cabinet there earlier.

After cleaning off the scratches with sterile cotton and hot water, Nancy prepared to paint them with iodine. "This may hurt a little," she said.

Tina had taken her fall bravely enough and, up until now, had shown no apprehension about the first-aid treatment. But as Nancy took the bottle of iodine out of the cabinet, the little girl suddenly lost her composure. She ran out of the stables with a look of fright on her face!

Puzzled and alarmed, Nancy capped the bottle and ran after her.

Assuming that Tina feared the pain of iodine on her open cuts, Nancy said soothingly, "Don't worry, dear. It won't hurt that much. Come on, we'll go in the house and find something else to treat those scratches with."

Mr. Harlow's maid brought another kind of antiseptic from a bathroom medicine cabinet. This time there was no flinching as it was applied. In fact, Tina scarcely noticed because she was so busy telling Nancy about the letter with a colorful foreign stamp on it that she had gotten from her mom and dad that morning.

The whole incident seemed trivial once it was over. Yet it bothered Nancy in a way she could not quite explain. It seemed to remind her of something else, perhaps something connected with the mysteries she was trying to solve. If only she could remember *what*!

Never mind, Nancy told herself. If it's really important, it will come back to me.

She had said good-bye and was just about to step into her car when Tina came running out of the house. "Nancy, Nancy! Wait!" she shouted. "There's a phone call for you!"

The pretty detective hurried back to the house. Tina led her into a side hall and pointed to a beige phone on a small table.

"Hello, Nancy," Carson Drew said. "One of my investigators just gave me some information that you'll be interested in. Do you have a pencil and paper handy?"

Nancy picked up a pen and notepad kept beside the phone. "All right, I'm ready, Dad."

"This concerns Pepper Nash, that jockey you asked me to have traced. It seems he's been living and racing in England since he left here. But he returned about the first of the month, and he's now living at 172 Hickory Court in River Heights!"

Nancy was startled. "Dad, that's great news!" she exclaimed. "Thanks a lot. I think I'll go talk to him right now. See you tonight."

"Good-bye, honey. Drive carefully," Carson Drew said and hung up.

Heading into town, Nancy turned this latest development over in her mind. The fact that Pepper Nash had returned to River Heights just before Shooting Star was stolen was bound to make him an even more likely suspect in the case.

She found him to be a slender, sandy-haired young man in his early twenties. He met her at the door and invited her into a small living room that looked comfortable but not very neat.

"Please excuse the disorder," he smiled. "I'm not too good in the housekeeping department."

Pushing a book out of the way, he sat down opposite Nancy. "Now, what can I do for you?" His blue eyes looked frankly into hers.

"I understand you've just returned from England," Nancy remarked. "Did you race over there?"

"I certainly did!" He quickly got up and brought her a large, leather-covered book from a shelf. "My scrapbook," he smiled. Opening it, he pointed out pictures and news reports of various races clipped from British papers.

Judging by the stories and photos, he seemed to be a winning jockey.

"Congratulations." Nancy smiled up at him. "You ought to show this to Roger Harlow."

"What do you mean?" Pepper's eyes narrowed.

"Oh, you know about that old dispute, do you?"

When Nancy nodded, he went on, "Well, part of my reason for coming back here was to clear up that misunderstanding. I know what he believed—that I threw that race—even though he didn't complain officially."

"But you knew how he felt?" Nancy inquired gently.

"I'll say I did! He made that very clear . . . really blasted me with both barrels! All the same, he was decent enough not to spread word around or try to give me a bad name. Someone else who overheard our quarrel did that."

Nancy said, "Now that you're back, what exactly do you intend to do?"

"Admit the truth to him, that I was a bullheaded know-it-all. You see, I thought the instructions he gave me for running the race were all wrong. He wanted me to hold back and take it easy at first, not really open up until the final stretch. Instead, I ran it my own way. I set a hot pace right from the start and lost—by two lengths! I was mad at myself, and Mr. Harlow's bawling out made me madder than ever. That's why I couldn't face the truth and take my medicine."

Pepper Nash began walking about the room. "I think I've grown up quite a bit since then. I'm going

167

to apologize and ask Roger Harlow for another chance. I want to clear my name with him."

"I hope you do," Nancy said earnestly.

As she got up to leave, he said in a puzzled tone, "We never got around to why you came to see me. Are you a reporter or what?"

Nancy smiled. "No, I'm trying to solve a mystery. Originally, I came to talk to you about a racehorse called Shooting Star. He's disappeared. But now I realize you couldn't have had anything to do with it."

An understanding expression came over Pepper Nash's face, and he smiled back ruefully at Nancy. "I read the news stories, of course, about him being stolen. But you're right, I know nothing more about it, and I certainly had nothing to do with the theft. I hope Harlow gets him back, though. From his record, Shooting Star sounds like a promising horse." He held the door open for Nancy and solemnly said good-bye.

Before going out to the Grimsby Mansion, Nancy decided to have a sandwich and milkshake at The Hangout. As she ate, she mused on her interview with the jockey. If nothing else, Nancy felt it had at least eliminated one suspect.

Soon she was on her way again, refreshed and looking eagerly forward to the afternoon's shooting at the mansion. This time, her only role would be that of spectator. Her own scenes were finished.

When she arrived, Ned came out to greet her, smiling happily. He told her that he expected to wrap up the project that afternoon, a whole day ahead of schedule. Everyone seemed in high spirits at the prospect, and things went smoothly.

In between scenes, Nancy went out to walk around a bit and enjoy the fresh air. The sun was shining down brightly through the treetops, and at this moment the only sign of past troubles were the blackened ruins of the burned-down stables.

Wisps of hay were scattered about nearby. This was not the first time she had noticed them. But suddenly Nancy stood stock still, struck by an idea. The old Grimsby Mansion had stood empty for years. Yet this was *fresh hay*, which meant a horse must have been stabled here recently!

Nancy's brain was in a whirl. Everything began falling into place.

A horse had been kept here recently. Of course! And that was precisely why the stable had been burned down. To keep the film club from discovering that very fact!

As for the silver bud vase and that missing painting, Nancy already knew they were items of loot from the country-house burglaries. And perhaps they were not the only such items to have been brought here. For some reason, the Grimsby Mansion must have served as a storage place until the loot was disposed of! But then the club members had spoiled it all by reopening the old house!

Was there any connection between the two halves of the puzzle?

Another thought flashed into Nancy's mind. What was it that had tantalized her earlier that day? Something she couldn't quite recall to memory. It had occurred to her after Tina's downhill fall when the little girl had been scared by the sight of that iodine bottle.

Suddenly, the final piece of the jigsaw clicked into place. All at once the young detective knew why Tina had been so frightened!

Impulsively, Nancy got into her car and set out for Rainbow Ranch. She was determined to get the full story from Tina!

19

Dusty Fur

When Nancy reached Rainbow Ranch, she left her car in the drive and rang the front door bell. The maid who answered said Tina had taken a book outdoors. "She's probably reading somewhere in back. Shall I come out and help you look for her?"

"No, thanks," Nancy said and smiled. "I'm sure I can find her."

As she expected, the little girl was ensconced in the pavilion, deeply absorbed in a story. But at the sight of Nancy, she jumped up eagerly and let the book fall from her lap. "Hi, Nancy! Did you come over just to see me?"

"How did you guess?" Nancy chuckled. She was relieved to find Tina in such a bright, cheerful mood. This might make a difference in her willingness to answer questions.

Nancy sat down on the ledge of the summerhouse and waited until the little girl was settled comfortably beside her. Then she took her hand and said, "I've come to tell you something, dear."

"Tell me what?"

"That I know what scared you about that iodine bottle this morning." Nancy paused before going on gently, "It was that skull and crossbones on the label, to warn people that iodine can be dangerous, wasn't it?"

Tina nodded without speaking.

Nancy slipped an arm around her. "And I think that reminded you of a live skeleton you once saw that scared you. Am I right?"

Tina's eyes had widened fearfully and her lower lip trembled as she murmured, "Y-Y-Yes."

"Believe me, honey, that wasn't a real skeleton," Nancy said quickly. "It was just a man in a black Halloween costume with a white skeleton painted on it!"

As if an emotional dam had broken, Tina burst into tears. In a moment, she was sobbing out the whole story. The little girl related that she loved her grandma's opal pendant and had tried it on one day when her grandpa was not at home. He knew of her fondness for the beautiful gem, and had warned her never to take it away from the dressing table where it was kept. But Tina had disobeyed him.

"I w-wore it out in the woods," she confessed between sobs.

Worse yet, she had decided to visit the old mansion that day, even though he had told her sternly never to play by herself in such lonely places. Tina, however, loved to indulge in make-believe, and the Grimsby Mansion with its court-yard and outlying stables and coach house seemed a marvelous place to imagine herself as queen of the castle.

On this particular day, much to her surprise, the front door of the mansion was partly open, and she heard a noise inside. Peeking in the window, Tina saw a stranger. "And he saw me, too!" she said shakily. "I was so scared, I ran away!"

Nancy guessed that the child had probably been as much embarrassed at being caught peeking as she was frightened. At any rate, as she turned and darted into the woods, the opal pendant had snagged on the bush and been torn off her neck!

Later, Tina lay awake all night long, feeling guilty over her double disobedience and worrying about what would happen when her grandfather discovered the jewel was missing.

"It was awful!" Tina said tearfully. "I just couldn't stay in bed. Finally, I got up and dressed real quietly. Then I tiptoed downstairs and sneaked out into the woods."

"You went back to the old house to get the pendant? All alone, in the dark?" As Tina gulped and nodded, Nancy hugged her close. "What a brave little girl!"

"B-B-But I *wasn't* brave! And that's when it happened!" Tina's voice broke.

"You saw the skeleton?"

"Y-Y-Yes! With an awful skull head! It came galloping up on a horse, right toward me! I was so scared. I screamed and screamed like anything, and ran home through the woods!"

The little girl's body was racked with sobs. Nancy rocked her back and forth, patting her soothingly. No wonder the poor little thing was so upset, the young detective thought, when I came galloping toward her that first day!

Aloud she said, "Just remember, dear, that wasn't really a skeleton. It was only a bad man dressed in a spooky costume just like boys and girls dress up on Halloween!"

When Tina was able to talk again, between sniffs and gulps, she related that after crawling back into bed and under the covers, she had had a terrible nightmare about the skeleton on horseback. And ever since, she had lived in constant fear of the day when her grandfather would discover her naughtiness.

"And maybe then the skeleton would come after me again!" Tina ended with a few more convulsive sobs.

"Don't worry, dear. That won't happen," Nancy said, trying to soothe her. "That bad man was a burglar, and the police are after him. When they catch him, he'll go to jail for robbing houses all around Brookvale Forest."

Now that Tina's crying had ceased, her curiosity was aroused. She looked up at Nancy with an expression of keen interest. "I d-didn't know burglars rode horses."

"This one did." Nancy smiled.

"Why?"

"Because there are police cars on the road at night, looking for robbers like him. That's why he always rode through the woods on horseback whenever he robbed a house—so the police wouldn't see him! Then he would stable his horse at the old mansion until the next night when he went out to rob another house."

"Oh!" Tina said anxiously. "Was the poor horse inside when the stable burned down?"

Nancy shook her head. "No, I'm sure it was taken away beforehand, because the robber found out a movie was being filmed there. Remember, I was going to take you there to watch?"

As the little girl nodded, Nancy went on, "As a matter of fact, I think Shooting Star was also kept in that stable after he was stolen. But he was taken away, too."

"Where?" Tina asked, wide-eyed.

Nancy shrugged regretfully. "I don't know yet. But I intend to find out! Meantime, let's wash those tear stains off your face, honey."

As they walked back to the house, Patches, the tortoise-shell cat, wandered past them. She sat down by the brook and began grooming her fur.

Nancy stopped short, her brain suddenly busy again. Another piece of the jigsaw had just clicked into place!

If Patches lived in the stables, perhaps she had actually *seen* the theft of Shooting Star! And on the day that she startled Bess's mount, she could have been on her way home from Grimsby Mansion! She had certainly been coming from that direction. In fact, if the horse or horses were still in the mansion stable that Saturday afternoon before the fire, Patches might have gone there on purpose to visit her old pal, or if she had not yet discovered where the thieves took the thoroughbred, perhaps she had been hunting for him and had just succeeded in snooping out his hiding place!

"What's wrong, Nancy?" asked Tina.

"Honey, do you have any idea where Patches was coming from just now?"

The little girl shrugged. "Gosh, I don't know. She wanders all over. Why?"

"I was told that she and Shooting Star were good friends and liked to be with each other. Is that right?"

Tina brightened and smiled. "Oh, yes! The stablehands used to say they could almost talk. It was fun to watch them!"

Nancy said earnestly, "You know what, Tina? I feel sure that Shooting Star wasn't taken very far away from here. If I'm right, maybe Patches knows where he is."

The little girl gasped excitedly. "Do you really think so?"

"Yes, dear, I do. Look at that white dust on her fur. Have you any idea where it might have come from?"

As they walked closer to the cat, Tina stared at it, then shook her head. Patches paused from licking her fur and regarded them with topaz-bright eyes.

"Wait!" Tina exclaimed suddenly. "I think I do know. I'll bet she got that at the old mine!"

"You've been there?" Nancy asked.

"Sure, lots of times until Grandpa told me not to go anymore, 'cause it might be dangerous. But I remember now, whenever I went there, I'd always come back with that funny dust on my shoes!"

Nancy knew about the mine Tina was referring to. She recalled Carson Drew mentioning once that zinc had been mined there. But she had never actually visited the site.

"Would you show me the mine?"

"Oh, yes! Especially if you think we might find Shooting Star!"

"How do we get there?" Nancy asked. "Just walk?"

Tina hesitated. "Well, we could but it's kind of far to walk. I only went there on my pony."

"Then suppose I drive us."

On their way to Nancy's car, they passed Kurt Ellum. The trainer gave them a curious stare, but only nodded curtly without stopping and touched his cap to Nancy before continuing on to the paddock.

The young sleuth did a sudden doubletake. She had just remembered what Ned found in the tree after the smoke bomb went off. And wasn't Ellum wearing *green* trousers?

Nancy shot a glance over her shoulder. Yes, she was right! But the trainer was too far away for her to see if there was any tear in them. Of course, the strand of material Ned had found snagged on the branch was fairly small, so the damage might be hardly noticeable. For that matter, Ellum might have had it mended by now. Nevertheless, Nancy decided to mention the matter to Police Chief McGinnis.

Meanwhile, there was a much more promising lead to follow up!

Moments later, Nancy's car sped away from Rainbow Ranch. The large estates bordering on Brookvale Forest were all situated on one side of the road. The opposite side was undeveloped—hilly and almost wild in places.

"Turn here!" Tina said. A rough, rutted dirt path led off the paved road. Nancy turned onto it as the little girl directed. But the path was so bumpy, she stopped.

"Is the mine much farther?" she asked.

"No, you can almost see it from here."

"Then let's get out and walk."

A large wooden door had once closed off the mouth of the mine. But it had rotted and fallen into disrepair over the years since the mine was abandoned, leaving an opening big enough for a person —or for that matter a horse—to get through.

Nearby was an ancient railroad siding. Nancy

179

guessed it had once led to the smelter. But that had been torn down long ago or perhaps lay out of sight beyond the hills. The entire area was now over-grown with tall weeds and brush.

As the two girls approached the mine, a slight breeze must have carried their scent ahead of them. A faint whinny suddenly sounded!

Tina gave a cry of excitement. "He's here!"

"It certainly sounds like it!" Nancy agreed.

They hurried forward. Nancy took a flashlight from her shoulder bag and led the way. She stepped through the opening, shining her beam of light into the dark mine tunnel. Not ten yards away stood a horse, tethered to one of the mine timbers. He neighed again, seeing his two visitors.

The horse was a dark chestnut stallion, obviously a thoroughbred. But as the girls came closer, they stopped in disappointment.

"That's not Shooting Star!" exclaimed Tina.

"I know. He has no white marking," said Nancy. Thoroughly puzzled, she walked up to the spirited animal, which gave an eager whinny and pranced several times with its forelegs. Nancy patted his neck to calm him.

Frowning, she said, "Could this be the horse that man in the skeleton suit was riding, Tina?"

The little girl shook her head decisively. "Oh, no!

180

That one wasn't a thoroughbred. And it was a pinto, I think. This one looks almost like Shooting Star except for the markings."

Suddenly, Nancy caught her breath. "You've just given me an idea, Tina!" Pausing for a moment, she went on, "Look, honey, do you feel brave enough now to ride this horse with me if I keep my arms around you?"

"I guess so—maybe," Tina replied in a small, squeaky voice.

Nancy hugged her. "Trust me, dear, please! We'll have to ride bareback, but I'm sure this fellow won't give us any trouble."

"All right."

Nancy untethered the thoroughbred and led it out of the mine. Then, standing on a rock ledge, she sprang nimbly onto the horse's back and lifted Tina up in front of her.

"Where are we going?" the little girl asked.

"That depends on the horse. I'm going to let him go his own way and hope he goes home. It may take a while, though. Are you still game?"

"I guess so," Tina replied. She sounded as though she were getting over her initial nervousness. "But what about your car?"

"It'll be safe for the time being, I hope." Nancy nudged their mount with her heels, clinging to his mane with both arms around Tina. The horse moved forward calmly as if sensing the person on his back was an experienced rider.

At first he meandered along, stopping from time to time to nibble on vegetation. But gradually he picked up speed and began to pace more steadily. "He's got his bearings now, I think," Nancy murmured.

Fifteen minutes later, he carried them onto the grounds of the Morston estate and headed for the stables! A groom emerged from the doorway. He was thin and sharp featured. Nancy recognized him as the man she had seen Morston talking to on her first visit to the estate.

He stopped in open-mouthed astonishment at the sight of the two bareback riders. Then his expression hardened. "What do you want?" he snapped as Nancy dismounted lithely and lifted Tina down.

"I've brought one of Mr. Morston's thoroughbreds home. I'll just see if his stall is open."

Before the groom could stop her, Nancy had darted past him into the stable! Tina followed. Most of the stalls were vacant, their occupants still outdoors. But in one stood a tall, dark chestnut stallion.

"That's *him!*" cried Tina. "That's Shooting Star!"

20

Star Bright!

"You're crazy!" the groom snarled. "Do you see any white markings on him?"

By this time, Nancy was close enough to the thoroughbred's stall to check with her own eyes. And the groom was right: his coat was a solid dark chestnut on both sides!

From the look on Tina's face, it was apparent that the little girl had just made the same discovery. The name sign on the horse's stall was BENBOW.

The groom said roughly, "Are you satisfied now?"

"No, we're not!" Nancy retorted.

He strode angrily toward the young sleuth, looking as if he were about to eject her by force. "Get out of here, both of you! Right now!"

Nancy's heart was pounding but she stood her ground. "Don't be absurd!" she said coldly. "I'm a friend of Mr. Morston. He told me I'm welcome here at any time. And I'm also a friend of Police Chief McGinnis!"

Her words brought the groom to a sudden stop. His face expressed his baffled rage. With a muttered oath, he turned and strode out of the stable.

Nancy, meanwhile, stroked the thoroughbred's neck and spoke to him soothingly. She could see that he was a high-spirited animal, but he responded at once to her calm, confident manner.

When she saw that he had accepted her, she opened the door to his stall, slipped inside, and began to take something out of her shoulder bag.

"What are you going to do, Nancy?" Tina asked anxiously.

"Try using some nail-polish remover and see what happens." As Nancy rubbed with a piece of tissue, a darkish stain began coming off the horse's left side. Underneath was a white marking!

"*It's Shooting Star!*" Tina squealed gleefully. "Oh, Nancy! You're so smart!"

"Yes, isn't she?" said a voice from the stable doorway. "Too smart for her own good, I'm afraid!"

As both girls whirled toward the speaker, they saw that Hugh Morston had just come in. He looked as trim as ever in a blazer and slacks with his suavely styled fair hair and pencil-thin mustache. But there was a nasty look in his eyes.

"I'm afraid you've made a bad mistake, my dear," Morston went on with a cold smile. "Now we can't let you leave here and tell your story to the police."

Nancy whispered something to Tina. The next instant, the young detective burst out of Shooting Star's stall and ran toward an open doorway at the far end of the stable!

"Stop her, Nate!" Morston yelled to the groom. He himself dashed down the alleyway between the two rows of stalls in pursuit of the fleeing girl.

Nancy came running out of the stable doorway and started around the corner of the building only to run straight into the arms of Nate! "Not so fast," he said, grabbing her arm.

Nancy struggled fiercely, calling on all the self-defense moves that her father and Ned had taught her. But when Hugh Morston joined in the fray, the two men soon overpowered her, each pinioning one arm!

"Where's the little kid?" Nate asked, staring all around, then blurted, "Hey, there she goes!" and pointed toward the woods. Tina could be seen disappearing among the trees in the direction of Rainbow Ranch.

185

Morston was furious when he realized that the child had seized her chance to escape during Nancy's dash for freedom. "Never mind!" he snapped. "Tie up this redhead while I go call Karp and Ellum! We can still handle this so there'll be no evidence or witnesses. But we'll have to work fast!"

Ellum! So Mr. Harlow's trainer was involved in the theft of Shooting Star! The news did not come as a total surprise to Nancy. She had already begun to suspect his role in another aspect of the mystery.

Nancy's wrists were quickly taped behind her back. Then Nate took her into the stable to guard her while his employer made two quick phone calls.

Morston returned grinning smugly.

"Any luck, boss?" Nate asked.

"Couldn't be better! Our problem will be over even sooner than I hoped!"

"Be sensible," Nancy said, looking Morston coolly in the eye. "Let me go at once or you'll end up in even worse trouble than you are in already!"

His answer was a chilling laugh. "Sorry, my dear. I have other plans. Kurt Ellum is about to start out through the woods on horseback from Rainbow Ranch. He'll pick up that little brat on the way and bring her back here to my place. Then, his friend Karp will dispose of you both."

"And who is Karp, may I ask?"

"You may," Morston chuckled, "since you'll never have a chance to tell your friend, the police chief. If you really want to know, Karp is a trucker and a close pal of Ellum's. They had a nice little racket going not long ago. But now they both take orders from me."

Nancy said shrewdly, "Did their racket, as you call it, happen to be country-house burglaries?"

"My, my! You *are* a smart girl, aren't you?" said Morston. "Yes, as you've rightly guessed, they're the ones who've been pulling all those robberies around here. Or rather Ellum was. Karp transported the loot to New York and fenced it. But Ellum made one bad mistake."

"Which put him in your power, I suppose."

"That's right. The fool tried to rob *my* house one night, just after I had it equipped with all the latest alarms and security devices. As a result, I caught him red-handed!"

Nancy's keen mind, skilled at unraveling mysteries, was already two jumps ahead of Morston's explanation. "And in exchange for not turning him in to the police," she said, "I presume you forced him to steal Shooting Star for you."

Hugh Morston looked astounded. "My dear, you really do impress me," he said. "No wonder you've gained such a reputation as a detective. When I saw

187

you in the library the other evening, I thought I could mislead you by pointing the finger of suspicion at Harlow's old business enemy, Howard Ainslee. But apparently my plan didn't work."

"Not for long, anyhow. And your plan for getting rid of little Tina and me won't work, either!" Nancy added defiantly.

"Don't count on that," Morston said and smiled. "Karp's on his way here from town in a tractor-trailer van. It should be pulling into the drive almost any minute now. When he leaves, you and your little friend will be in it along with my chestnut stallion Benbow. If you'll forgive me for saying so, Miss Drew, you really should keep your pretty little nose out of other people's business. This time, it's gotten you into serious trouble!"

"You can't keep us in a van forever!"

"Too true, sweetie. I fear we shall have to arrange some sort of accident."

The unpleasant conversation was interrupted as Nate reported the arrival of the van. Morston beckoned Karp, who was at the wheel, to drive it up to the stable. The groom then loaded the chestnut stallion Benbow into the van.

By this time, Morston was pacing up and down fretfully. "What's keeping Ellum?" he muttered.

"Here he comes now!" Nate exclaimed. The trainer was just galloping out of the woods on the white Arabian, Snowflake. But he was alone.

"What's wrong with that stupid clod?" Morston fumed. "He was supposed to pick up the kid!"

"It's not his fault," Nancy spoke up unexpectedly. "You see, Tina didn't really run home through the woods as you thought."

"*What?*" Hugh Morston glared at his captive with a puzzled smile.

"I told her as soon as she was out of sight of your place to head for the road and try to signal for help," Nancy explained. Then she added with a smile and a tilt of her head, "You've all been so busy watching Kurt Ellum, I don't think you've noticed that a police car just turned up your drive. Tina's probably inside it."

There was a moment of wild panic as Morston and his accomplices saw that Nancy was telling the truth. But they soon realized that they were trapped and that fight or flight was useless. They could only watch sullenly as the police car braked to a stop and two uniformed officers got out with their hands on their weapons. Seeing Nancy with her wrists bound, the officers promptly arrested the four criminals, who were quickly handcuffed.

Tina had been waiting in the back seat of the scout car. But now she jumped out and embraced her friend while one of the policemen was untaping the young detective's wrists. "Oh, Nancy! I'm so glad you're all right!" the little girl exulted.

"Thanks to you, dear," Nancy responded. "Did you have much trouble getting help?"

"I did at first. But then a lady stopped and picked me up. She drove me along until we found a police car."

Nancy was asked to accompany the prisoners to police headquarters. It was dinnertime before she was able to return home. That evening, Ned and Bess and George all came over to the Drew house to hear the full story after a television news flash reported that the stolen thoroughbred Shooting Star had been found.

"Whatever made someone as rich as Morston commit such a crazy crime?" George asked.

"Actually, he wasn't all that rich," said Nancy. "His advertising business was failing. So he joined a syndicate with Judd Bruce and another man to buy the racehorse Minaret. They entered it in the River Heights Handicap and Morston bet heavily on their horse to win. But when Shooting Star was also entered, he got frightened. If Minaret lost, he would be ruined."

190

"So he had to get rid of the one horse that might beat him," put in Ned.

"Exactly. And that one horse was Shooting Star." Nancy explained how Morston had forced Kurt Ellum to steal the thoroughbred from Rainbow Ranch. Ellum had drugged Alf Sanchez's coffee and switched thermoses after the watchman passed out. Then he rode Shooting Star to the Grimsby Mansion stable, where he was already keeping the pinto that he used in committing the country-house burglaries.

"So when Ned's film club arranged to shoot the movie at the mansion, it must have thrown those crooks into an awful tizzy!" Bess said.

"It certainly did," Nancy replied. Both Ellum and his accomplice Karp had made full confessions in the hope of receiving lighter sentences, so she was now able to fill in many details.

Karp had a criminal record before going into the trucking business. An expert at cracking safes and locks, he had fashioned a key that enabled Ellum to use the old mansion as a central base for his burglaries. By riding horseback, he was able to rob houses all around the Brookvale Forest area, and then make his getaway without any risk of being seen by police patrol cars.

Karp had actually been lurking in the mansion

when Ned first came to look it over with Mr. Ullman. By eavesdropping, he had heard of the movie project.

"So the horses had to be hastily removed from the mansion stable before the filming started," Nancy went on. "Karp took away Ellum's pinto, and Shooting Star was moved to the old mine. But Morston didn't like leaving a prize racehorse in such an exposed place, especially since he hoped to sell it later in South America. So he had Star switched with one of his own thoroughbreds, Benbow, who wasn't particularly valuable."

Nancy added that Morston had been planning the switch for some time. This was the real reason why he had fired Lou Yelvey, who might recognize the prize stallion, and replaced him with the crooked groom, Nate, who was willing to aid his criminal scheme.

Meanwhile, Ellum and Karp knew that a silver bud vase, one of the items of loot, had been lost at the mansion and were afraid the film club might find it. They were also hoping to resume the burglaries, using the carriage house rather than the stable as a hiding place for Ellum's horse. For both reasons, they did their best to drive the college group away from the old house.

Karp was the one who had marked the warning

on the dusty table top and later stretched the wire across the cellar stairs. He had also sneaked into the mansion one night to remove the stolen painting, which he and his partner had overlooked.

Ellum had left the threatening note on Nancy's car. Later he had crayoned the warning on her windshield and also tossed the smoke bomb into the mansion, hoping to get the club members evicted.

Two weeks later, after solving the mysteries at Rainbow Ranch and the old Grimsby Mansion, Nancy and Tina were Roger Harlow's guests as they watched Shooting Star win the River Heights Handicap. And that weekend, the young detective and Ned, along with Bess and George and their dates, attended the film club festival in New York City at which the contest entries were to be shown and judged.

Ned's comic vampire movie brought down the house with laughter and won first prize. He and the famous girl sleuth, Nancy Drew, who had starred as the film's heroine, were asked up on the stage to receive the award.

"Nancy didn't just star in my movie," Ned told the audience. "She uncovered some real crooks in the house where we did the filming. Without her detective work, we couldn't have made the film at all."

Now that the movie was finished, Nancy wondered where her next mystery would lead. To her surprise, she would soon find herself in Florida on the trail of *The Sinister Omen.*

In the meantime, though, she blushed deeply as the audience and judges broke into applause. Ned slipped an arm around her and bent to kiss her cheek.

"You're my favorite movie star, Nancy," he said.

NANCY DREW® MYSTERY STORIES By Carolyn Keene

THE TRIPLE HOAX—#57	69153	$3.50	_____
THE FLYING SAUCER MYSTERY—#58	65796	$3.50	_____
THE SECRET IN THE OLD LACE—#59	69067	$3.50	_____
THE GREEK SYMBOL MYSTERY—#60	67457	$3.50	_____
THE SWAMI'S RING—#61	62467	$3.50	_____
THE KACHINA DOLL MYSTERY—#62	67220	$3.50	_____
THE TWIN DILEMMA—#63	67301	$3.50	_____
CAPTIVE WITNESS—#64	62469	$3.50	_____
MYSTERY OF THE WINGED LION—#65	62681	$3.50	_____
RACE AGAINST TIME—#66	69485	$3.50	_____
THE SINISTER OMEN—#67	62471	$3.50	_____
THE ELUSIVE HEIRESS—#68	62478	$3.50	_____
CLUE IN THE ANCIENT DISGUISE—#69	64279	$3.50	_____
THE BROKEN ANCHOR—#70	62481	$3.50	_____
THE SILVER COBWEB—#71	62470	$3.50	_____
THE HAUNTED CAROUSEL—#72	66227	$3.50	_____
ENEMY MATCH—#73	64283	$3.50	_____
MYSTERIOUS IMAGE—#74	64284	$3.50	_____
THE EMERALD-EYED CAT MYSTERY—#75	64282	$3.50	_____
THE ESKIMO'S SECRET—#76	62468	$3.50	_____
THE BLUEBEARD ROOM—#77	66857	$3.50	_____
THE PHANTOM OF VENICE—#78	66230	$3.50	_____
THE DOUBLE HORROR OF FENLEY PLACE—#79	64387	$3.50	_____
THE CASE OF THE DISAPPEARING DIAMONDS—#80	64896	$3.50	_____
MARDI GRAS MYSTERY—#81	64961	$3.50	_____
THE CLUE IN THE CAMERA—#82	64962	$3.50	_____
THE CASE OF THE VANISHING VEIL—#83	63413	$3.50	_____
THE JOKER'S REVENGE—#84	63426	$3.50	_____
THE SECRET OF SHADY GLEN—#85	63416	$3.50	_____
THE MYSTERY OF MISTY CANYON—#86	63417	$3.50	_____
THE CASE OF THE RISING STARS—#87	66312	$3.50	_____
THE SEARCH FOR CINDY AUSTIN—#88	66313	$3.50	_____
THE CASE OF THE DISAPPEARING DEEJAY—#89	66314	$3.50	_____
THE PUZZLE AT PINEVIEW SCHOOL—#90	66315	$3.95	_____
THE GIRL WHO COULDN'T REMEMBER—#91	66316	$3.50	_____
THE GHOST OF CRAVEN COVE—#92	66317	$3.50	_____
NANCY DREW® GHOST STORIES—#1	46468	$3.50	_____

and don't forget...THE HARDY BOYS® Now available in paperback

THE HARDY BOYS® SERIES   By Franklin W. Dixon

NIGHT OF THE WEREWOLF—#59	62480	$3.50	_____
MYSTERY OF THE SAMURAI SWORD—#60	67302	$3.50	_____
THE PENTAGON SPY—#61	67221	$3.50	_____
THE APEMAN'S SECRET—#62	69068	$3.50	_____
THE MUMMY CASE—#63	64289	$3.50	_____
MYSTERY OF SMUGGLERS COVE—#64	66229	$3.50	_____
THE STONE IDOL—#65	62626	$3.50	_____
THE VANISHING THIEVES—#66	63890	$3.50	_____
THE OUTLAW'S SILVER—#67	64285	$3.50	_____
DEADLY CHASE—#68	62447	$3.50	_____
THE FOUR-HEADED DRAGON—#69	65797	$3.50	_____
THE INFINITY CLUE—#70	69154	$3.50	_____
TRACK OF THE ZOMBIE—#71	62623	$3.50	_____
THE VOODOO PLOT—#72	64287	$3.50	_____
THE BILLION DOLLAR RANSOM—#73	66228	$3.50	_____
TIC-TAC-TERROR—#74	66858	$3.50	_____
TRAPPED AT SEA—#75	64290	$3.50	_____
GAME PLAN FOR DISASTER—#76	64288	$3.50	_____
THE CRIMSON FLAME—#77	64286	$3.50	_____
CAVE IN—#78	69486	$3.50	_____
SKY SABOTAGE—#79	62625	$3.50	_____
THE ROARING RIVER MYSTERY—#80	63823	$3.50	_____
THE DEMON'S DEN—#81	62622	$3.50	_____
THE BLACKWING PUZZLE—#82	62624	$3.50	_____
THE SWAMP MONSTER—#83	49727	$3.50	_____
REVENGE OF THE DESERT PHANTOM—#84	49729	$3.50	_____
SKYFIRE PUZZLE—#85	67458	$3.50	_____
THE MYSTERY OF THE SILVER STAR—#86	64374	$3.50	_____
PROGRAM FOR DESTRUCTION—#87	64895	$3.50	_____
TRICKY BUSINESS—#88	64973	$3.50	_____
THE SKY BLUE FRAME—#89	64974	$3.50	_____
DANGER ON THE DIAMOND—#90	63425	$3.50	_____
SHIELD OF FEAR—#91	66308	$3.50	_____
THE SHADOW KILLERS—#92	66309	$3.50	_____
THE BILLION DOLLAR RANSOM—#93	66310	$3.50	_____
BREAKDOWN IN AXEBLADE—#94	66311	$3.50	_____
DANGER ON THE AIR—#95	66305	$3.50	_____
WIPEOUT—#96	66306	$3.50	_____
CAST OF CRIMINALS—#97	66307	$3.50	_____
SPARK OF SUSPICION—#98	66304	$3.50	_____
DUNGEON OF DOOM—#99	66309	$3.50	_____
THE HARDY BOYS® GHOST STORIES	50808	$3.50	_____

NANCY DREW® and THE HARDY BOYS® are trademarks of Simon & Schuster, registered in the United States Patent and Trademark Office.

AND DON'T FORGET...NANCY DREW CASEFILES® NOW AVAILABLE IN PAPERBACK.

JAMIE GILSON KEEPS YOU LAUGHING!